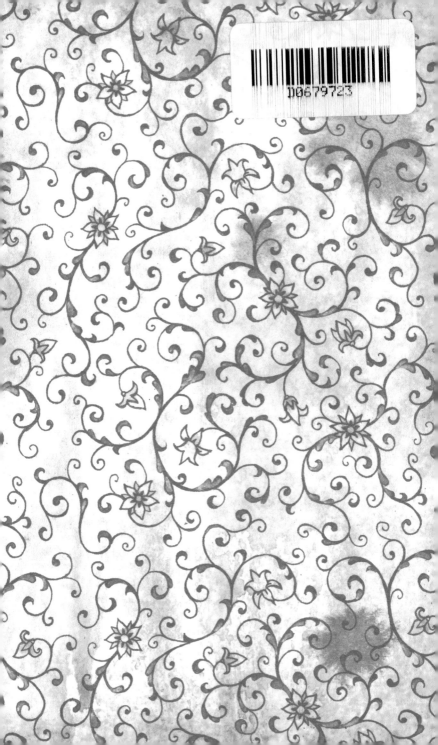

Wakestone
Hall

Books in the Stella Montgomery series

Withering-by-Sea

Wormwood Mire

Wakestone Hall

A Garden of Lilies: Improving Tales for Young Minds

Wakestone Hall

A Stella Montgomery Intrigue
by Judith Rossell

ABC
Books

The ABC 'Wave' device is a trademark of the
Australian Broadcasting Corporation and is used
under licence by HarperCollins*Publishers* Australia.

First published in Australia in 2018
by HarperCollins*Children'sBooks*
a division of HarperCollins*Publishers* Australia Pty Limited
ABN 36 009 913 517
harpercollins.com.au

HarperCollins*Publishers*
Level 13, 201 Elizabeth Street, Sydney NSW 2000, Australia
Unit D1, 63 Apollo Drive, Rosedale, Auckland 0632, New Zealand
A 53, Sector 57, Noida, UP, India
1 London Bridge Street, London SE1 9GF, United Kingdom
2 Bloor Street East, 20th floor, Toronto, Ontario M4W 1A8, Canada
195 Broadway, New York NY 10007, USA

A catalogue record for this book is available
from the National Library of Australia

ISBN 978 0 7333 3820 5 (hardback)
ISBN 978 1 4607 0818 7 (ebook)

Cover and internal design by Hazel Lam, HarperCollins Design Studio
Cover and internal illustrations by Judith Rossell
Typeset in Bembo by Kirby Jones and Kelli Lonergan
Printed in China by RR Donnelley

5 4 3 2 1   18 19 20 21

For Chren, with many thanks

One

$\mathcal{S}$tella Montgomery awoke from a frightening dream. Something was chasing her. Swooping down from the dark sky. A pale creature with papery wings, reaching with long, cold, spindly fingers that snagged in her hair and clutched at her neck.

Shaking, Stella took a shuddering breath and then another one. She sat up and looked around. For a moment, she did not recognise anything at all.

It was a low room with a sloping ceiling. Iron beds were lined up in two rows with a narrow space between them. Fifteen beds in all. Each bed had a small dressing table beside it and a hook for a washbag. At one end of the room was a doorway, and at the other end was a large wardrobe and a small window. Stella could hear someone snoring, someone else sniffing and the rain pattering on the roof.

She was in the First Form dormitory at Wakestone Hall Select Academy for Young Ladies. She was at school.

Stella shivered, pulled the thin blanket around her shoulders and wrapped her arms tightly around her knees. Her heart was still thumping, as if she had been running for her life. She could still feel the flapping creature's cold, clutching fingers.

She rested her chin on her knees, took another deep breath and tried to cheer herself up by thinking about something encouraging. But it was very difficult, because Wakestone Hall was dreadful. Of course, any boarding school chosen by the Aunts was certain to be unpleasant, but Wakestone Hall was even worse than Stella had imagined it would be. The mistresses were strict, the lessons were long and tiresome, and the food was horrible.

There were sixty other girls here, more girls than Stella had seen in her life before. She had hoped that she would make friends, but the girls were oddly subdued. They filed along the passageways of the school in silence and kept their eyes down during lessons. Stella was one of the youngest girls, and she felt very insignificant and lonely. Even one friend would make everything better.

She missed her cousins. But they had sailed away

with their father and their governess, to look at seaweeds in the Sargasso Sea, and Stella did not know when she would see them again. She wished she could have gone with them, but instead the Aunts had insisted she be sent back to live with them at the Hotel Majestic at Withering-by-Sea.

One afternoon, as the Aunts were sitting in the long sunroom of the hotel, wrapped up like three puddings, still emitting little wisps of vapour from the wave bath, sipping glasses of murky, greenish water and eating cakes, Aunt Deliverance had unexpectedly announced that they had decided to send Stella to boarding school.

'Discipline,' Aunt Deliverance said. She poked a cocoa-nut macaroon into her mouth and chewed it decisively. 'Strict discipline.'

'Rules and retribution,' Aunt Temperance said, as she sipped her glass of water, her wandering eye rolling around in an irritated manner.

'Yes, indeed,' agreed Aunt Condolence. Her Particular Patent Corset creaked and twanged as she swallowed a piece of plum cake.

All three Aunts glared at Stella.

'Wakestone Hall is an excellent school,' said Aunt Deliverance. 'A good situation. Not far from our old home, Wormwood Mire.'

'Deliverance was Head Girl,' said Aunt Temperance proudly. 'And she won the Needlework Prize and the Etiquette Prize and the Elocution Prize. And Countess Anstruther's Correct Conduct Medal.'

'Three times,' said Aunt Condolence, simpering.

And then, quite unexpectedly, the Aunts started to sing. They had remarkably high, quavering voices.

Wakestone Girls, through toil and strife,
Marching sternly throughout life.
Striding through the darkest night,
Always Righteous, Always Right.

It was a long song with many verses. There were twitters of surprise from the other residents. General Carruthers grumbled into his moustache; Lady Clottington's nasty little dog, Sir Oswald, gave a shrill howl of distress and shot underneath her chair. Stella felt her toes curl up inside her shoes with astonishment. She had to bite her tongue to stop herself from giggling. Surely, the Aunts had never been schoolgirls. It was impossible.

'Your late mother was at Wakestone Hall too, of course,' said Aunt Deliverance. 'She behaved unforgivably.' She frowned. 'Despite this, Miss Garnet has agreed to take you, as a particular favour to me. I trust you will be grateful and obedient.'

'Yes, Aunt Deliverance,' said Stella, sounding as grateful and obedient as she could manage. She had never thought about her mother at school. What had she done that was so dreadful? It was no use asking the Aunts. They never answered her questions.

Perhaps it would be interesting to go to the school her mother had attended, so many years before.

Three weeks later, Stella had found herself arriving at Wakestone Hall for the start of the new term. She was stiff and awkward in her new clothes. Her coat and dress were made of a scratchy fabric. Her new boots were tight and pinched her feet. The stockings were itchy, and the underclothes were complicated and uncomfortable. On her hat was a ribbon in the school colour for Wakestone Hall, a spiteful shade of purple.

She arrived at the school as evening was falling, and her first impressions were of a confusing maze of echoing dark passageways and cold, shadowy rooms.

There were two other new girls in the First Form: Agapanthus Ffaulkington-Ffitch and Ottilie Smith. Stella had hoped they might become friends, but neither of them seemed particularly agreeable. Agapanthus looked to be about the same age as Stella. She had freckles and her wiry, gingery hair was twisted into two twig-like plaits that stuck out from her head. She seemed bad-tempered, and when Stella had given her a quick smile, Agapanthus had only scowled briefly in return.

Ottilie was a year or so younger and the smallest girl in the whole school. She was thin, with black hair and dark eyes. She was timid and nervous, and when Stella had smiled at her, she had looked so startled that Stella had been afraid that she would burst into tears.

They had been together for nearly two weeks, but they were no closer to becoming friends. Every day, Stella sat beside Agapanthus and Ottilie for lessons (Elocution, Etiquette, Household Management, French Conversation and Needlework, all equally unpleasant). Each afternoon, they walked together at the end of the long, silent line of girls that filed into the town to visit the Wakestone Municipal Gardens on fine days, or the Wakestone Museum when it was raining, which it generally was. They slept side by side in the dormitory.

It would have been easier to make friends if they had been able to talk, but at Wakestone Hall, the girls were only permitted to speak to one another at mealtimes, and a mistress sat at the head of each table, to ensure that their manners were faultless, and that their conversation was of an elevating nature and in French.

Miss Mangan, the First Form mistress, was very strict and immaculately neat. She sat as rigid as a poker and her pale eyes gleamed behind her spectacles, alert for mistakes. Despite many years of lessons with Aunt Temperance, Stella knew how to say only the simplest things in French — certainly she could not manage anything elevating — and so she just concentrated on not attracting Miss Mangan's attention, and ate her way miserably through bowls of plain porridge, which tasted rather like glue, cold mutton with boiled cabbage, bony fish pie with watery white sauce, dry bread with a scrape of margarine, and heavy suet pudding drowning in thin, lumpy custard.

Stella sighed, feeling dispirited.

Usually, whenever she needed to comfort herself, she thought about her sister. It was always encouraging to think of Luna. She often dreamed about her. In her dreams, she became Luna. Slipping silently through the trees in the wood at night, or singing softly in the moonlight, or sometimes flying through the dark sky on the back of an enormous owl.

But tonight, there had been a frightening, clutching creature in her dream. What did that mean? Was Luna in danger? It was a horrible thought. Stella wished there was a way she could be sure that Luna was sleeping safely in Mrs Spindleweed's sweetshop at Wormwood Halt. It was not very far away. Stella wished she could send her a message. *Be safe*, she whispered silently. She imagined the words, like tiny, flickering candle flames. Perhaps Luna was dreaming of her, and she would hear the message in her dream.

Stella shivered. What would Agapanthus and Ottilie, or any of the girls at Wakestone Hall, think if they knew she had a twin sister who was invisible? Or that she could sometimes turn invisible herself? That she was fey? She was determined that they would never discover her secret.

She thought about the last time she had seen Luna. It had been at night, in the middle of a wood. She remembered Mrs Spindleweed standing in the moonlight, holding her shawl tightly around her shoulders and saying fiercely, *I've kept her safe, all this time. And I will now.*

She had made Stella promise that she would keep Luna a secret. Then she had transformed into an owl and flown away, with Luna riding on her back.

'You would hate it here,' she whispered to Luna, in the darkness. 'You would hate it even more than I do.'

She heard a muffled sob. It came from Ottilie, in the next bed. Stella could see only a dark shape huddled under the bedclothes. She opened her mouth to whisper something, and then hesitated.

No girl shall Converse with Another, after Lights Out, for any Purpose whatsoever.

There were many rules at Wakestone Hall. There were lists of them pasted up on a wall of every dormitory and classroom, and the new girls had to learn them by heart. If a girl broke a rule, she was made to copy it out many times, in perfect handwriting. There were so many rules that it was remarkably easy to get into trouble without even realising it. Stella had already spent several evenings sitting in the cold classroom, copying out the rules she had broken, while all the other girls were having supper, or darning their stockings and listening to one of the mistresses read an improving story from *The Young Ladies' Magazine and Moral Instructor.*

Girls who misbehaved were sent to the Headmistress's parlour. Stella had not yet caught sight of the Headmistress, Miss Garnet, and she did not know exactly what happened in her parlour, but that only made the prospect more dreadful. The previous week, one of the new girls from the Third Form had been sent to the parlour. When she had returned an hour later, she had looked pale and shaken, and had not spoken at all for two days afterwards.

In the darkness, Ottilie gave another hiccupping sob.

Stella whispered, 'Are you all right?'

Ottilie did not reply.

Stella whispered again, 'Please don't cry.'

The only answer was a sniff.

Stella felt a bit discouraged, but she tried once more. 'It's dreadful here. But perhaps —'

A sudden sound startled her. Stella froze, listening.

It was probably the matron, Miss McCragg. She had a wooden leg and used a stick, so she made a clumping sound as she walked. She wore a starched white apron and lurched like a frightening battleship around the passageways of Wakestone Hall at night, inspecting all the dormitories to make sure no girl was awake or out of bed.

Stella heard it again. It was a scrabbling sound. But it did not come from the passageway; it came from the window.

Excepting in the Advent of an Emergency, no girl shall Arise from her Bed before the Waking Bell.

Stella took a breath, glanced at the door, and then climbed out of bed. The linoleum felt like ice under her bare feet and she shivered. She hugged her arms around herself as she crept past Ottilie's bed to the window.

Every Dormitory Window shall be opened by precisely Two Inches to prevent the Accumulation of Noxious Miasmas.

Stella cautiously pulled the window further open and leaned on the sill, looking out at the cold, rainy night.

From the narrow attic window, the steep roof sloped down to an iron gutter. The tall houses around the school made jagged black shapes against the night sky. Four storeys below, the wet cobblestones glimmered in the light of the street lamps.

The clock on the town hall began to strike. Stella counted the distant chimes. Twelve o'clock. Midnight.

She heard the scrabbling sound again. Just below the window, a dark shape was moving on the roof. Stella almost shrieked. Then the shape gave a squeaking mew, and she gasped with relief. It was a cat, clinging to the slippery slates. It mewed again.

'Don't fall,' whispered Stella. She leaned out of the window and tried to grab the cat, but could not reach far enough. She climbed up onto the windowsill, stretching out as much as she could. The cat tried to scramble up the roof towards her. Stella leaned out a bit further. Her heart lurched as she felt herself overbalance. There was nothing to hold on to. Her fingers slid on the wet slates. She was going to topple headfirst out of the window. She gave a squeak of terror.

Someone gripped her around her middle.

'I've got you,' whispered a voice. It was Ottilie.

'Hold tight,' gasped Stella. She took a steadying breath, reached down as far as she could and managed to grab a handful of fur on the cat's neck. 'Got him.'

Ottilie heaved, and Stella wriggled backwards, dragging the cat with her. She climbed down from the windowsill, wet and shaking, holding tightly to the struggling cat.

'Thank you,' she whispered.

Ottilie nodded.

The cat scrambled up onto Stella's shoulder. He dug his claws in with enthusiasm and made several happy mewing sounds. Clearly, he was delighted to be inside and out of the rain.

'*Shhh*,' Stella whispered, stroking him. He was a darkish colour, black or grey, with gleaming round eyes. She could feel his bones under his shaggy, wet fur. His claws were like needles.

'What will we do?' she asked Ottilie. 'He'll wake everyone up, and we'll be in so much trouble.' There was sure to be a rule about having a cat in the dormitory. There were probably several rules about it.

She was certainly breaking half-a-dozen rules, right now, all at once.

The cat miaowed again, loudly and unhelpfully, and bit her ear, quite hard. Stella stifled a squeak. One of the sleeping girls muttered something and turned over, but did not wake up.

Ottilie stroked the cat's head. 'P-poor cat. He's hungry.'

'I'm sorry, cat,' Stella whispered, 'but you can't stay here.' She stroked him again as she considered what to do. 'I think I will take him downstairs. Perhaps I can open a window and put him out.'

'I could come with you, if you like,' whispered Ottilie nervously.

Stella said, 'If we get caught, we'll be in so much trouble.'

Ottilie hesitated, and then nodded.

Stella thought about Miss McCragg. What if she came in while they were gone? 'We should push our pillows under the blankets. Like this.' A bit awkwardly, Stella passed the wriggling, protesting cat to Ottilie. Stella bunched up her blanket and pushed her pillow underneath. Ottilie returned the cat to her and did the same to her own bed. The cat clambered up onto Stella's shoulder again. Ottilie gave her blanket a few tweaks and pats. They stood back. From a distance, in the darkness, it might fool Miss McCragg, if she did not look too closely.

Stella took a breath. 'Let's go,' she whispered.

Then they tiptoed to the door and looked out into the passageway.

Stella swallowed. There were many dangers to pass. There were two other dormitories along the passageway, a washroom and a row of maids' bedrooms. On the floor below were three more dormitories, and below again were the mistresses' rooms and classrooms. Below that, and most terrifying of all, they would have to go right past the door to the parlour of the Headmistress, Miss Garnet.

They would have to be very careful, and very lucky, and as silent as mice.

'Come on,' Stella whispered.

The two girls crept out into the passageway. There was a clumping sound and a gleam of candlelight. The cat dug his claws into Stella's shoulder and hissed.

Ottilie clutched Stella's arm. 'Oh no!' she whispered.

A huge shape loomed into view at the end of the passageway.

Miss McCragg was approaching.

Two

'Quick!' gasped Stella.

They fled back into the dormitory and dashed towards their beds. In the darkness, Stella collided with the end of a bed. Ottilie bumped into her. The cat miaowed indignantly.

'Who's that?' Agapanthus sat up in the bed and grabbed the sleeve of Stella's nightgown.

'Let go! Miss McCragg's coming,' Stella whispered desperately.

The clumping footsteps were getting closer. Candlelight glimmered.

Agapanthus whispered, 'Quick. Under the bed.'

Stella and Ottilie dropped to the floor and scrambled underneath Agapanthus's bed. The cat wriggled and hissed.

'*Shhh*,' said Stella, gripping him tightly around his middle.

They were just in time. The huge shape of Miss McCragg appeared in the doorway. The flickering light from her candle made the shadows stretch across the floor. Stella held her breath. She could feel Ottilie trembling. Just above their heads, Agapanthus gave an unconvincing snore.

Miss McCragg grunted something and progressed into the dormitory. She passed so close that Stella could have reached out and touched her skirt. Miss McCragg's apron crackled. Had she noticed the empty beds? She reached the open window, and the girls heard her mutter in an annoyed manner. Then they heard a squeak as she pushed the open window down to exactly two inches. She turned and clumped back out of the room.

Her footsteps receded.

Agapanthus whispered, 'Wait,' and she climbed out of bed, tiptoed to the door and looked out into the corridor. She came back, poked her head under the bed and whispered, 'She's gone.'

They crawled out and stood up.

'Thank you,' said Stella.

'What are you doing with that cat?' asked Agapanthus.

'He came in the window,' said Stella.

'Poor cat.' Agapanthus patted him. The cat miaowed loudly.

'I think he's hungry,' whispered Ottilie.

'We're taking him downstairs, to let him out,' said Stella.

'I'll come with you,' said Agapanthus.

'If we get caught, we'll be in so much trouble,' whispered Stella.

'Of course. So we won't get caught.' Agapanthus sounded impatient. She quickly pushed her pillow under her blanket and gave it a pat. 'Come on,' she said.

They tiptoed to the door again and peered out at the dark passageway, listening.

After a moment, Stella whispered, 'Let's go.'

They slipped out of the dormitory and crept along in single file, keeping close to the wall. Stella led the way, carrying the cat, followed by Ottilie and then Agapanthus. They reached the end of the passageway and started down the staircase. The stairs creaked. They crept down slowly, step by step.

On the floor below, they tiptoed past another row of dark doorways.

Clumping sounds approached. Candlelight flickered.

'It's her again. Quick!' whispered Stella.

They dashed into a dormitory and flattened themselves against the wall behind the open door. The cat mewed again and butted his head against Stella's ear in a friendly manner.

'*Shhh*,' whispered Stella. She felt for his face in the darkness and put her hand over his mouth.

Miss McCragg's footsteps came closer and stopped. They could hear her breathing and smell her, a strong scent of coal-tar soap, cod-liver oil and brimstone.

She muttered something under her breath, and then her footsteps clumped away along the passageway. After a few seconds, Agapanthus looked around the door and whispered, 'She's gone.'

They tiptoed to the stairs and made their way down, passing the mistresses' bedrooms and the classrooms. They went on until they reached the passageway that led past the Headmistress's parlour. They stopped and peered around the corner. Dim light filtered in from a window, making shadows on the floor.

Ottilie hesitated.

'Come on,' whispered Agapanthus.

The cat mewed.

'*Shhh*,' whispered Stella.

Silently, they crept along the passageway and slipped, one by one, past the door of Miss Garnet's parlour. They came to the top of an imposing, tiled staircase. Below, in the middle of the entrance hall, was a table holding a large, dusty aspidistra in an enormous brass pot. Light shone in from the gas lamp in the street outside, making the coloured glass in the window above the front door glow and sparkle.

'Not this way,' whispered Ottilie, clutching Stella's arm.

'No,' agreed Stella.

No Girl Shall Traverse the Main Staircase under Any Circumstances.

This was the first rule Stella had learned at Wakestone Hall. She had broken it within ten minutes of arriving, and she had spent her first evening at school writing it out fifty times as neatly as she could while trying not to cry.

The girls turned and went along the winding passageway that led to the back stairs.

The cat mewed again.

'He's hungry,' whispered Ottilie. 'Perhaps we can find him something to eat.'

'We might find something in the kitchen,' said Stella, as they made their way down the back stairs. 'There might be leftovers from dinner. There was that fish pie. And that jam pudding.'

'That fish pie was utterly horrible,' whispered Agapanthus crossly. 'It was full of spiky bones, and it tasted like mouldy socks. We can't give that to the poor cat. Of course not. And that jam pudding looked just like the flabby leg of a dead man. I hid my piece in my pocket, and I threw it out of the window. It's probably still lying right there in the flowerbed. I bet even rats wouldn't eat it. The food here is utterly revolting.'

Stella and Ottilie giggled.

Agapanthus pushed open the door to the dining room, and they threaded their way between the long tables. 'This school is utterly dreadful. I'd like to put slugs in the mistresses' stockings. I put a toad in my governess's bed once. You should have heard her scream. The kitchen must be through here.'

She pulled open the green baize door, and they followed her along a tiled passageway, down a short flight of stairs, around a corner, and found themselves in a cavernous, shadowy room that smelled of grease and old boiled cabbage. A large table was covered with pots and pans and piles of plates and bowls. There was an enormous range, and high up on one wall was a row of small windows. One of them was open, and the rain was coming in.

Ottilie opened several drawers and cupboards and peered inside. 'There's nothing to eat here,' she whispered.

Agapanthus lifted the lid of one of the giant saucepans on the range. 'Empty,' she said. 'Where's the larder?'

Stella spied a door, close to where they had come in. It had a latch and a padlock. 'Here, I think.' She rattled the padlock. 'But it's locked.'

The cat gave a hungry mew.

'Poor cat, there's nothing for you here,' said Stella, stroking him.

Ottilie touched the padlock with her finger, and then she held it between her hands. There was a tiny click from inside, and she pulled it open and unlatched the door.

'How did you do that?' asked Stella, surprised.

Ottilie hesitated. 'It wasn't locked,' she said.

The larder was a dark, narrow room, lined with shelves and full of sacks and barrels and boxes. Agapanthus searched along the shelves, cautiously poking her fingers into things. 'Lard,' she said. 'Flour. Oatmeal.'

Ottilie lifted the cover from a bowl and smelled the contents. 'Prunes, I think.' She picked up a plate and had a sniff. 'Oh, I think these are Miss Garnet's sausages.'

Miss Garnet often had sausages with fried bread for breakfast, or a haddock sometimes, or mutton chops, or devilled kidneys. She always had something that smelled delicious. Her grim, elderly maid carried her meals through the

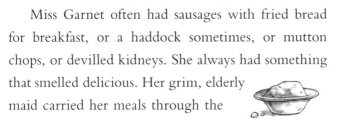

dining room and up to the parlour on a special silver tray.

Agapanthus prodded the sausages. 'There's a whole string of them. Do you think she'd notice if one was gone?'

'I bet she would,' said Stella.

The cat made a sudden happy growling sound. He wriggled out of Stella's grasp and leaped at the sausages.

Ottilie squeaked, stepped backwards, tripped and dropped the plate. It shattered on the tiled floor with a crash that sounded like a thunderclap.

'Oh no!' she gasped.

The cat pounced on the string of sausages and pulled them into a corner behind a big sack of onions. Stella knelt down and groped around behind the sack, trying to reach the sausages. The cat hissed and took a swipe at her. She jumped back. The sack toppled, and the onions bounced and rolled across the floor.

The cat shot out from his hiding place. Stella tried to grab him, but she stepped on an onion, lost her balance and collided with Agapanthus. The cat clambered up to the highest shelf of the larder, taking the sausages with him. A large tin toppled down.

'Ouch!' squeaked Ottilie, who was crawling

around underfoot, picking up bits of broken plate and scattered onions.

'I'm sorry!' whispered Stella. She climbed up the shelves and felt along the top for the cat. 'Puss, puss,' she crooned. He hissed at her again and darted away along the shelf, dragging the sausages. Another tin fell down with a clang.

'*Shhh*. Someone's coming,' whispered Agapanthus.

Stella gasped.

Ottilie gave a little shriek.

There was no time to escape. Agapanthus tried to pull the larder door shut, but it would not close properly.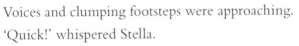

Voices and clumping footsteps were approaching.

'Quick!' whispered Stella.

They scrambled to the back of the larder and crouched there together, behind a big sack of potatoes.

Candlelight gleamed around the edges of the larder door.

They were trapped.

Three

The footsteps came closer and the larder door was flung open.

Miss McCragg stood in the doorway. She held a candle in one hand and brandished her stick in the other. Two nervous-looking maids peered around from behind her.

At the back of the larder, behind the sack of potatoes, Stella felt Agapanthus flinch. Ottilie was shaking.

'Who's hiding in there?' Miss McCragg waved her stick above her head. 'Come out at once!' She advanced into the larder.

Stella felt for Ottilie's hand in the darkness and gripped it tightly.

If Miss McCragg took one more step, she would see them.

At that moment, Miss McCragg stepped on an onion. She screeched and waved her arms around, dropping the candle. It sputtered and went out. She staggered backwards, out of the larder, knocking a pile of bowls from the table. They hit the floor with a smash.

The maids shrieked.

The cat yowled. He shot down from the shelf and out of the larder with his tail like a bottlebrush, trailing the sausages behind him. Miss McCragg flailed around in the darkness, trying to hit the cat with her stick. She missed him, but knocked over another pile of crockery.

The maids squealed.

The cat bounded up on the table and leaped onto Miss McCragg's head. She screeched again, swinging wildly with her stick, bashing into things. Several saucepans fell down, clanging. Miss McCragg tripped over a saucepan and thumped into the maids. They all fell over.

The cat sprang up onto a high shelf, and from there up onto the windowsill. He shot out of the open window, disappearing into the night, along with all of Miss Garnet's sausages.

Stella nudged Agapanthus and Ottilie and whispered, 'Come on. Quick.'

They crept out of the larder.

They tiptoed around Miss McCragg and the maids, as they untangled themselves and struggled to get to their feet.

Miss McCragg saw them and shouted, 'Who is that? Stop there!'

They did not stop. They sprinted out of the kitchen as fast as they could go, down the passageway, up the stairs and through the dining room towards the back stairs.

Ahead, candlelight flickered.

Stella halted so abruptly that Agapanthus collided with her and nearly knocked her over. 'Someone's coming down!' she gasped. They spun around and sped back the way they had come.

As they ran back past the door of the dining room, another crash echoed from the kitchen. Miss McCragg shouted. Ottilie squeaked in terror. They dashed towards the entrance hall.

A figure was coming down the main staircase carrying a lamp. Just in time, they flung themselves behind the brass pot that held the aspidistra. The Senior Mistress, Miss Feldspar, stalked past them. She wore a dressing gown and a lace nightcap. If she had turned her head, she would have seen them hiding, but fortunately, she did not.

They waited for a second, glanced at one another, and then crept from their hiding place and bolted up the main staircase, taking two stairs at a time. They sprinted along the passageway past Miss Garnet's parlour, around the corner and up the stairs. As they ran past the mistresses' bedrooms, a door handle rattled.

'No!' gasped Agapanthus.

The door opened and Miss Mangan's head poked out. She looked very peculiar, with a knitted nightcap covering her hair, cold cream covering her face, and without her spectacles or her teeth.

Ottilie shrieked, tripped and fell over. Stella and Agapanthus grabbed her hands and pulled her to her feet.

Miss Mangan peered out at the dark passageway, blinking short-sightedly. 'Who's there?' she asked.

Stella and Agapanthus dragged Ottilie around the corner and up the stairs. They sprinted along the passageway, climbed the final, winding staircase and tiptoed along the narrow passageway to the First Form dormitory.

It was quiet on the top floor of the school. Rain pattered on the roof. Far below, they could hear faint voices and distant thumps and bangs. There were murmurs in the other beds. Someone turned over and went back to sleep. Nobody had followed them. Nobody woke up.

Stella took a gasping breath as she climbed into her bed. She pulled the blanket up to her chin. 'We made it,' she whispered.

'I think Miss McCragg saw us,' said Ottilie. 'Or Miss M-Mangan. I think Miss Mangan saw us.'

'I'm sure they didn't,' said Agapanthus. 'It was too dark. And we were too fast. And Miss Mangan didn't have her spectacles on, anyway.'

After a moment, Ottilie whispered, 'I hope the poor cat got away.'

'He did. I saw him jump out the window,' said Stella.

'He's belting down the road right now, with all of Miss Garnet's sausages,' whispered Agapanthus, and she gave a sudden snorting laugh.

When the rising bell clanged early the next morning, Stella felt as if she had been asleep for only a few minutes.

Her dreams had been confusing and frightening, and her head felt thick and heavy. She yawned and rubbed her eyes. Dim morning light filtered in from the window. It was still raining, and it was very cold.

The dormitory maid, a cheerful girl, hurried into the room with a pile of folded towels. She whispered, 'Get up, she's coming,' pulled a face and added over her shoulder, 'And she's in a right old bate this morning, so she is.'

Stella clambered out of bed, shivering. She yawned again.

'Up, up,' said Miss McCragg, clumping into the dormitory. She was leaning heavily on her stick. There was a nasty-looking scratch on the side of her face. 'Get up, there.' She banged her stick against the ends of the beds. 'Inspection today.' She stamped over to the first bed, pulled open the drawers of the dressing table and poked her stick inside.

'She's looking for sausages, I bet,' whispered Agapanthus.

Stella's heart gave a lurch. Hidden in the bottom drawer of her dressing table was a little musical box. It had once been her mother's. She had brought it to school because she could not bear to leave it behind with the Aunts at the Hotel Majestic. She had tucked it right at the back of the drawer, behind her summer vests and stockings, but it was a poor hiding place, and if Miss McCragg found it, she would confiscate it.

Keepsakes and Ornaments are Vulgar and Sentimental and Strictly Forbidden.

The matron was coming closer, moving briskly through the dormitory, searching every bed and dressing table. She poked a mattress and a pillow, then upended a drawer, spilling hair ribbons and stockings onto the floor. She stirred them around with the end of her stick, snapped, 'Tidy that up,' and moved on to the next bed.

As soon as Miss McCragg's back was turned, Stella knelt down, pulled open her bottom drawer and snatched out the musical box. She clutched it to her chest.

'Where can I hide this?' she asked in a desperate whisper.

'Up the leg of your drawers,' suggested Agapanthus.

'It's too big.'

'Under your pillow?'

At that moment, Miss McCragg flung a pillow across the room. Stella gasped.

Ottilie whispered, 'P-put it in your washbag. I know somewhere. I'll show you.'

Miss McCragg had reached Agapanthus's bed and was prodding the mattress in a suspicious manner.

Stella snatched her washbag off its hook and crammed the musical box inside, along with her sponge and her hairbrush. She drew the string closed. The bag looked rather lumpy. She bundled her towel over her arm and hoped Miss McCragg would not notice.

She was just in time. Miss McCragg clumped over and yanked open the drawers of Stella's dressing table. She stirred the contents around, frowning. She poked under the pillow, prodded the mattress, and then moved along to Ottilie's bed. Stella let out the breath she had been holding.

They hurried along to the washroom. The older girls were looking nervous.

'Someone was out of bed. In the kitchen. In the night.'

'It's against the rules. There'll be trouble.'

'*Shhh*,' hissed one of the girls, looking anxiously over her shoulder. 'No talking.'

Stella, Agapanthus and Ottilie exchanged a look.

'They didn't see us,' said Agapanthus under her breath, as they washed their hands and faces in the icy water. 'Of course not. Nobody saw us.'

Ottilie looked around to make sure none of the big girls were watching them, and then she nudged Stella and beckoned her into the lavatory stall at the end of the row. 'Quick,' she breathed.

Stella slipped into the stall, and Ottilie shut the door and ducked down behind the lavatory, peeled back the linoleum, poked her fingers into a knot hole and lifted up a floorboard. Underneath was a small cavity, where the pipe from the lavatory went down under the floor. It was a perfect hiding place. It already contained a little toy rabbit, made of felt and embroidered with coloured silk.

'See,' whispered Ottilie, pointing into the cavity. 'I found it. It's safe, I think. You can share it, if you want. There's room.'

'Thank you,' whispered Stella. She took the musical box out of her washbag and placed it in the cavity, beside the rabbit.

Ottilie stroked the rabbit with the tip of her finger. 'My m-mother made him for me when I was little,' she said. 'It reminds me of her —'

The dressing bell clanged, making them both jump. Ottilie pushed the floorboard down and flattened the linoleum back into place. They rushed back to the dormitory. Stella took off her nightgown and pulled on clean drawers, chemise, stays, stockings and petticoat, twisting around to do up the buttons and tie the tapes. She pulled the dress on over her head and buttoned it up as quickly as she could. The collar and cuffs were attached with hooks and tiny bone buttons, and they were all very fiddly, and her fingers were numb with cold. She managed to do them up at last, and then she brushed her hair and plaited it and tied the ends of the plaits with ribbon. She pushed her feet into her house shoes and tied the laces.

The breakfast bell rang, and everyone hurried to stand in line. Miss McCragg stood at the top of the stairs and inspected them as they filed down to the dining room. She looked furious. She rapped a girl on the head. 'Go back and brush that hair,' she said. She twitched a collar flat with a jerk that almost pulled the girl off her feet. She poked her stick at the shin of a girl with a wrinkled stocking, making her squeak. Stella and Agapanthus and Ottilie were last of all. Miss McCragg glared at them as they passed, but all she said was, 'Hurry up,' and tapped her stick on the floor impatiently.

Downstairs in the dining room, the kitchen maids were dumping big platters of bread and jam and chipped, mismatched plates onto the tables. There were little outbreaks of whispering all around the room. Usually, jam was a treat allowed on Sundays, and only then if a girl's conduct had been impeccable, and she had been sent a pot from home.

'No horrible porridge today, because all the bowls were smashed,' whispered Agapanthus, as they took their places, standing behind their chairs.

'*Silence, filles,*' said Miss Mangan, clapping her hands. The French mistress, Mlle Roche, struck a chord on the piano, and they sang the school song.

Wakestone Girls, so straight and true,
Always do as we should do.
Marching on with main and might,
Always Righteous, Always Right.

'*Asseyez-vous,*' said Miss Mangan.

Stella eyed the mistress nervously. Under cover of the sound of the chairs being pulled out, she whispered, 'She doesn't know it was us.'

'I hope not,' breathed Ottilie.

'Of course not,' said Agapanthus.

Stella's plate had a gilt rim and a pattern of fat pink roses, which was cheering. She helped herself to a slice of bread and jam. The jam was strawberry, her favourite. She felt her spirits rise a bit. Perhaps, after all, they would not be found out.

But just as they were finishing breakfast, Miss Feldspar, the Senior Mistress, stood up and said, 'Girls. Your attention.' Stella felt her heart jump. Agapanthus drew in a breath through her teeth. Ottilie choked on a mouthful of bread and jam.

Miss Feldspar was tall, with iron-grey hair and a

bony, arched nose, like the beak of a vulture. Her lips were set in a thin line. She said, 'Several girls were out of their beds last night, and were so far lost to propriety as to venture into the kitchen and purloin comestibles.' She paused to allow her cold gaze to sweep the room. 'These girls have broken fourteen separate rules. Fourteen. As well as a significant amount of crockery. They will come forward immediately. Miss Garnet wishes to see them in her parlour.'

There was a rustle of nervous whispering. Girls turned to look at each other.

Stella glanced sideways at Agapanthus and Ottilie. Agapanthus was scowling, and Ottilie looked frightened.

'Silence!' snapped Miss Feldspar.

There was an instant hush. Stella looked down at the roses on her plate and swallowed. Nobody spoke.

At last, Miss Feldspar said, 'Believe me. There will be far worse consequences if the girls responsible do not come forward right now.' She waited one more moment. 'Until they do, the whole school will be punished. There will be bread and water for supper, and complete silence at all meals.'

As they joined the end of the line of girls that filed out of the dining room after breakfast, Ottilie shot a glance over her shoulder and breathed, 'W-what will happen if they find out?'

'I don't know. Something truly horrible,' whispered Stella. She shivered.

'They won't find out,' whispered Agapanthus, frowning. 'Of course not.'

Four

Wakestone Hall was a tall house that had once been home to a large, wealthy family. When it had been turned into a school, the grand rooms had been divided up to make a maze of classrooms and dormitories. The large drawing room had been turned into three classrooms. The First Form classroom was the smallest of these. It contained the enormous marble mantelpiece from the drawing room. There was never a fire in the fireplace, and when it was windy, the chimney howled in a hoarse and gloomy manner.

The classroom was dark and cold, and it smelled of mildew and chalk dust. The only pictures to look at were an engraving of the Queen, over the fireplace, and an oil painting of a ruined castle, near the door. There was a blackboard at the front of the room, a clock on the mantelpiece, a list of rules pasted to the wall and a small library consisting entirely of

old issues of *The Young Ladies' Magazine and Moral Instructor*. (Stella had looked through them, hoping to find something to read. They contained recipes and household hints, fashion plates, embroidery patterns, etiquette advice, court gossip from about twenty years ago, sentimental poems about fairies, and long, dreary serial stories that went for pages and pages without much happening at all.)

The first lesson every morning was Elocution. The girls in the First Form stood beside their desks and curtsied as Miss Mangan stalked into the room. She wrote *Discipline and Resolution Strengthen an Indifferent Constitution* on the blackboard, took a metronome from her desk drawer, wound it up with a little silver key and set it ticking.

She turned to the class and said, 'Feet together. Toes out. Shoulders back. Heads up.'

One by one the girls repeated the phrase in time with the ticking metronome, until Miss Mangan was satisfied with their pronunciation and their posture. Stella managed to say the words correctly on her third attempt, but she was scolded for slouching. Agapanthus was corrected for scowling and mumbling. Poor Ottilie was last of all, and she had to say the phrase again and again, her stammer getting a little bit worse each time, until she was incoherent and in tears.

'Clear enunciation and elegant deportment are the hallmarks of a gentlewoman,' said Miss Mangan crisply, as she wound up the metronome again.

Ottilie nodded, sniffed and said, 'Yes, M-M-Miss M-Mangan.'

The next lesson was Etiquette. Miss Mangan read out etiquette advice from *The Young Ladies' Magazine and Moral Instructor*, and the girls copied it into their notebooks. Seventeen incorrect uses for a fish fork. Instructions for how to address a letter to the second son of a baronet. Directives about exactly when one should leave a visiting card with a new acquaintance of a slightly lower social standing than one's own. Miss Mangan walked around the room, inspecting their work. She glared at the spots and smudges of ink in Agapanthus's book, tore the page out, crumpled it up and let it drop into the waste-paper basket.

'Again,' she said.

'Yes, Miss Mangan,' muttered Agapanthus, frowning as she dipped her pen into the ink.

The third lesson of the morning was Needlework, which was taken by Mlle Roche, the French mistress. They were learning to make button holes, and Mlle Roche insisted on tiny, perfectly even stitches.

Stella tried to make the stitches as neat as she could, but her fingers were cold, and the thread got tangled, and her work soon became crumpled and grubby.

'*Abominable*,' said Mlle Roche, examining it with distaste. She flung it back to Stella. '*Impardonnable*. You will begin again.'

'Yes, Mlle Roche,' said Stella with a sigh, as she began to unpick the stitches.

At last, the dinner bell rang. Stella stood up with relief, curtsied to Mlle Roche and followed the rest of the First Form as they filed out of the classroom.

Dinner was boiled tripe and cabbage. This time, Stella's plate had a chipped gilt rim and a cheerful decoration of several men on horseback galloping stiffly after a long line of hounds. Each mouthful of tripe she swallowed uncovered another horseman or another hound, and eventually, as she gulped down the last soggy bite, she discovered that they were all chasing a frisky-looking fox around the plate. The tripe was followed by a slice of suet pudding. It had cloves stuck in it like the bristles on the back of a hog, and it was wallowing in a pool of lumpy custard on a saucer that was decorated with forget-me-nots and daisies.

As Stella scraped up the last claggy bit of custard from her saucer, Miss Mangan announced, 'This afternoon we shall be visiting the museum, as the weather is inclement.'

In the cloakrooms, the girls changed from their house shoes into their boots, and pulled on their coats and gloves and hats. They pushed their sketchbooks and pencil boxes into the pockets of their coats, and lined up, two by two, in the entrance hall, in order of height. Prunella Gridlingham, the tall Head Girl, was at the front of the line. Stella, Agapanthus and Ottilie were at the end. Ottilie was the smallest, and she would have been last, all by herself, but they were permitted to walk together, because Miss Mangan thought it was tidier.

'Backs straight. Eyes down. Hands folded. In silence,' instructed the mistresses, as they stalked along the line of girls. Miss Feldspar drew back the bolts and opened the big front door, and they all filed down the steps and out into the drizzling rain.

Stella felt her spirits rise as they left the school. The mistresses walked closely beside them, making sure that nobody whispered or dawdled or turned their heads to gaze around, but even so, it was agreeable to be outside, and there were always things to see. Dead leaves and scraps of paper whirled along the street. Crows flapped overhead in the blustery, icy wind. A grocer's boy dawdled along, swinging a basket and whistling. A maid emptied a dustpan out of an attic window.

Agapanthus nudged Stella's arm and jerked her head. The cat from the night before was dashing across the street. He stopped and stared at them, then trotted towards Stella in a cheerful manner with his tail pointing straight up. In the daytime, Stella could see he was a handsome cat. He had grey fur with swirling black stripes and bright green eyes, but his whiskers were bent and his ears were tattered, as if he had been in many fights. He looked so pleased with himself that Stella giggled. She remembered how he had leaped onto Miss McCragg's head, and then shot out of the window with Miss Garnet's sausages trailing behind him. He had no idea of all the trouble he had caused.

'Silence!' snapped Miss Mangan, who was walking just behind them, holding a big umbrella. She slapped Stella on the head. 'Silence. Eyes down.' She flapped her hand at the cat. '*Shoo!*' she said, and the cat hissed at her with his ears flat on his head and dashed away.

They turned the corner into the High Street and made their way past the long row of elegant shops. Stella liked watching the carriages and carts and omnibuses trundling along, splashing through the muddy puddles.

In the shop windows, the flaring gas lights sparkled on rolls of brocade and lace and velvet, ornamented with tiny, glittering beads, and fashionable hats, decorated with birds, artificial grapes and flowers, and shining satin ribbons.

People hurried past, muffled up in their coats. Well-dressed children clutched their nurses' hands, and other children sold matches or flowers, or darted through the busy traffic, carrying packages and baskets, and running errands.

Halfway along the street, Ottilie gave a sudden frightened gasp and nearly tripped over her feet.

'What is it?' whispered Stella.

'N-nothing,' stammered Ottilie, glancing nervously back over her shoulder.

'Silence!' said Miss Mangan.

Stella looked back to see what had startled Ottilie. A heavily built man was leaning against a railing, picking his teeth as he watched the girls walk past, his dark eyes gleaming. He wore a shabby leather waistcoat and a bowler hat, and he had a red-and-yellow spotted handkerchief tied around his neck. He held a pot of paste and a brush, with a bundle of posters over his arm. At the top of the posters was a picture of a galloping horse.

Stella glanced at Ottilie again, but her head was down, and her face was in shadow.

Miss Mangan rapped Stella on the head. 'Eyes front,' she said.

At the end of the High Street they came to Museum Square. In the middle was the Memorial Fountain. On one side were the curly iron gates that led to the Wakestone Municipal Gardens and on the other side was the museum. It was a large building, with a row of columns and two large stone lions out the front, and a number of little sooty domes on its roof, like a collection of pepper-pots. The schoolgirls filed up the wide stone stairs and went inside.

Stella liked visiting the museum. There were glass cabinets of rocks and bones, and collections of rusty swords and arrowheads and broken statues. Overhead dangled the skeleton of an enormous creature with many pointed teeth.

Miss Feldspar frowned as she folded up her dripping umbrella. 'Begin work, girls. In silence, if you please.'

Stella pulled off her wet gloves and rubbed her cold hands together. She took her sketchbook out of her pocket, opened it up and gazed around to find something to draw. But before she could begin, Agapanthus grabbed her wrist and pulled her behind a cabinet, out of sight of the mistresses.

'What is it?' Stella whispered.

'Follow me,' whispered Agapanthus. She jerked her head at Ottilie, who was standing nervously nearby.

'What? Why?' asked Stella, but Agapanthus did not answer. She led them away from the main room of the museum, up some stairs and through a smaller room full of broken clay pots. Halfway up another flight of stairs was a narrow doorway, which led into a small round room with a domed glass ceiling. There were cabinets around the edges of the room, containing preserved seabirds and several models of ships and the teeth of whales and an anchor covered with barnacles. In the middle of the room was an enormous, overstuffed walrus. It had patchy, moth-eaten fur and beady glass eyes. It was so immensely fat, it looked as if it had swallowed a sofa. A sign on the wall read: *Specimens collected by the Expedition of the HMS* Perilous, *1768, commanded by Captain Archibald Winterbottom, FRS. All Lives Lost.*

Agapanthus looked around to make sure they were alone, then whispered, 'I found this room the other day. Nobody comes in here, because of the smell. And they won't hear us, because of the rain.'

It was true. The fat walrus emitted an unpleasant odour of mildew and camphor, which would have made anyone reluctant to linger, and the rain on the glass dome overhead made a steady sound that would muffle a whispered conversation.

Agapanthus eyed the fat walrus's glassy stare, opened her sketchbook and licked the tip of her pencil.

'So now we can talk,' she said.

Five

'I'm sure they don't know it was us last night,' Agapanthus said, frowning at the fat walrus as she began to draw a large, lumpish shape in her sketchbook. 'If anyone had seen us, we would already be in trouble. We'd have been sent to Miss Garnet's parlour, and I'm sure whatever happens in there is utterly dreadful. So we have to keep quiet about it, or it will be absolutely disastrous. Do you agree?'

Stella said, 'Yes,' and Ottilie nodded.

'Good,' said Agapanthus. She drew two little beady eyes on her walrus.

Stella sighed as she drew the outline of the walrus. 'It's horrible at school, isn't it? Perhaps we will get used to it, do you think?'

'I utterly refuse to get used to it,' said Agapanthus crossly. 'I knew it would be dreadful. I told my grandmother I would hate it, and I was right. It's utterly ghastly.' She frowned and added spiky whiskers to her walrus. 'I'd put a cockroach in Miss Mangan's corset, if I got the chance. That'd make her yell. Have a toffee.' She rummaged in the top of her stockings and pulled out a handful of sweets. She gave them one each. 'I smuggled them in here in the leg of my drawers. Don't let Miss Mangan see them. It's my grandmother who decided to send me to school. It's her fault entirely. How did you land here?'

'Thank you,' said Stella, as she unwrapped silver paper from the toffee and put it in her mouth. It was hard and round and tasted of treacle. 'I have Aunts.' Stella sucked the toffee. 'Three Aunts. They were at school at Wakestone Hall themselves, years ago. My mother too. She was the youngest sister. But I think she did something dreadful when she was here.'

'What did she do?' asked Agapanthus with interest.

'I don't know. My Aunts just said that it was something unforgivable. I'd like to find out. But they never answer questions. My Aunts are very disapproving of her.' Stella sighed again as she drew the whiskers on the walrus. 'And truly, that doesn't mean much, because they disapprove of everything.'

'Your Aunts sound just exactly like my grandmother,' said Agapanthus. 'They would get along very well. She adores disapproving of things. They would be absolutely the best of friends and have a marvellous time disapproving of things together. She utterly disapproves of me. She said I was thoroughly ungovernable.' Agapanthus pulled a face. 'Thoroughly ungovernable,' she repeated with angry relish. 'Mainly because I galloped on the gardener's pony through the great hall and up the grand staircase. One of the stable boys bet me that I would not do it, and so I did. But Mother had an attack of vapours, and she was absolutely prostrated for two weeks. So Grandmother came to stay, and she kept springing questions at me all the time. At breakfast, she'd say, "What are the principal exports of Bavaria, Agapanthus? How would you address an archdeacon, Agapanthus? Who is the king of Sweden, Agapanthus?" Of course, I knew absolutely none of the answers. None at all. Not one. And she said that I was thoroughly ignorant, and the governess was doing nothing with me, and I had better go away to school, so she sent me to Wakestone Hall.' She frowned and sucked her toffee and stabbed her pencil at her drawing, scribbling some patchy fur along the back of her walrus. 'Do either of you have any sisters or brothers?'

Ottilie shook her head.

Stella started to say, 'I have a —' But she stopped.

She had promised that she would keep Luna a secret. She bit her lip.

Fortunately, Agapanthus did not notice her hesitation, or wait for an answer, but went right on in an angry whisper, 'I've got six sisters. Six.' She counted on her fingers. 'Rose, Violet, Lily, Hyacinth, Zinnia, Gardenia. Mother named us after flowers. She thought it would be picturesque. Mother is artistic.' Agapanthus rolled her eyes. 'But when I came along, of course, she had utterly exhausted all the flowers she could think of. So she just opened the flower book and shut her eyes and jabbed it with a pin. And the pin landed on Agapanthus. Which is idiotic, of course. It is an utterly dreadful name, don't you think?'

'Well, it could have been worse,' said Stella, remembering her botany lessons with her cousins' governess. 'The pin might have landed on Toadflax. Or Hellebore.'

'Or Sneezewort,' whispered Ottilie.

'Yes. Or Bogbean,' agreed Agapanthus, pulling a face.

Stella and Ottilie giggled, and Agapanthus went on, 'My sisters are all very old. Rose and Violet and Lily are married already. And Hyacinth and Zinnia and Gardenia are out, which means they look at dress patterns and have their hair curled and put lemon juice on their freckles to make them disappear, which does not work at all, by the way, and they go to dances so they can meet someone eligible and get married too. It's utterly stupid. I shall never get married. Will you?'

Stella had never thought about getting married. 'I don't know,' she said doubtfully. 'I don't —'

'Silence, girls!' They all jumped. Miss Mangan appeared in the doorway. Stella nearly swallowed her toffee. She pushed it to the side of her mouth with her tongue and hoped the mistress would not notice.

Miss Mangan stalked around the fat walrus. 'What are you doing in here? I trust you are not wasting time with idle chatter. Show me your work.' She held out her hand impatiently, took their sketchbooks and inspected their walrus drawings. Stella's looked like a hairy potato with whiskers. Agapanthus had drawn the fur on her walrus with such force that it resembled a deranged pincushion. And Ottilie's drawing was so tiny that it looked more like a garden slug than anything else.

'Remarkably poor, indeed,' said Miss Mangan. 'There is considerable room for improvement.'

'Yes, Miss Mangan,' they said together, their voices slightly muffled because of the toffees.

'Sketching is an elegant and unobjectionable occupation for a gentlewoman,' Miss Mangan said.

'Begin again.' She stood over them, watching them work for several minutes. Then she sniffed and said, 'In silence,' and went away.

Agapanthus waited until Miss Mangan was gone, sucked the toffee and went on with her story, 'Everyone in the family wanted me to be a boy, especially Father. I was his last hope, and I am a ghastly disappointment to him. He is always away in the city, because he cannot bear to look at me. And Mother lies on her divan all day. She is unwell with nerves and artistic notions.' Agapanthus made an exasperated sound. 'I knew school would be utterly dreadful. And it is, isn't it?'

'Yes,' agreed Stella.

Ottilie started to say something, and then stopped. She took a breath and started again. 'There was only M-Mother and me. Just the two of us together. And we were happy. We were. We had a little shop here in Wakestone. A locksmith shop. I helped mother in the shop, and she taught me my lessons. But then she went away —' She hesitated and said in a tiny, miserable whisper, 'Something dreadful happened. M-my mother is gone. And so now there is only me. I was sent to school, because there is nowhere else for me to go. I would run away, I think. If I was b-brave enough. And if there was somewhere for me to run away to. But there is nowhere.' Her voice quavered. She sniffed, and a tear trickled down her face. She wiped it away with the back of her hand.

Stella patted Ottilie's arm. 'I am sorry.'

'That's dreadful,' said Agapanthus, frowning.

Stella said, 'My mother is dead too, but she died when I was little. I don't really remember her at all. But it won't be so bad if we can be friends. We can look after each other, don't you think?'

Ottilie sniffed again and nodded.

'Of course we can,' said Agapanthus. 'Let's shake on it.' She put out her hand. Stella took hold of it, and after a moment, Ottilie did too. They gripped their three hands together.

'Friends,' said Stella.

'Yes,' said Agapanthus. 'We should make a pact, don't you think? We should swear on something.' She looked around the room.

'Let's swear on the walrus.'

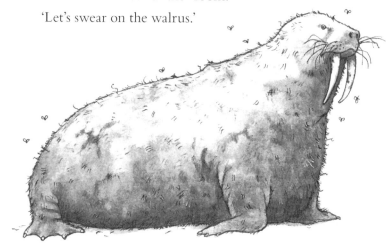

In an impressive voice, she said, 'I swear on this fat walrus that we three will be true friends, and always help each other at this utterly horrible school.'

Stella giggled and repeated, 'I swear on this fat walrus.'

Ottilie did not say anything, but she clutched their fingers tightly and gave them a tiny smile.

It was raining heavily by the time they left the museum, and they hurried back along the High Street, heads down, huddled in their coats, struggling against the icy wind, their boots slipping and sliding on the wet cobblestones.

Stella shivered as they trailed back into the cold classroom. The first afternoon lesson was Household Management. How to remove ink stains from velvet, tallow stains from ivory, Macassar oil stains from mother-of-pearl and blood stains from mahogany.

Stella stood beside her desk and waited for her turn to repeat the lesson. She supposed it was useful to learn about removing stains. Perhaps when she returned to live with the Aunts, they would be impressed with her new stain-removing abilities, and also with all the other things she was learning at school about fish knives and visiting cards and button holes, and they would be pleased with her.

She sighed. It seemed extremely unlikely. She glanced at Agapanthus, who was frowning, and Ottilie, who gave her a quick, nervous smile.

Certainly, school would be more bearable now she had two friends.

The classroom was freezing. Her toes felt like ice. She wriggled them inside her shoes, and behind her back she rubbed her cold fingers together.

There was a knock at the door. The Headmistress's elderly, grim-faced maid stalked into the room and muttered something to Miss Mangan.

Miss Mangan looked up. 'Ottilie Smith,' she said. 'Miss Garnet wishes to see you in her parlour.'

Everyone gasped and turned around to gape at Ottilie.

Ottilie gave a startled squeak. 'M-me?' she faltered. 'But —'

'Do not keep Miss Garnet waiting,' said Miss Mangan.

Ottilie seemed to be frozen with fright. She glanced desperately at Stella and Agapanthus.

'Ottilie,' snapped Miss Mangan.

Ottilie swallowed, bobbed a curtsy, and then followed the maid out of the room.

Stella looked at Agapanthus.

'Eyes front,' said Miss Mangan.

Ottilie did not return during that lesson, or the next lesson, which was French Conversation with Mlle Roche (where they were learning how to make remarks about the weather), or during Preparation (where they were learning a long, sad poem by heart).

Stella sat at her desk and stared at her lesson book, but she could not concentrate on learning the sad poem, because she kept thinking about Ottilie. What was happening to her? Had someone found out about the sausages?

The poem was about a lady who was pining for a gentleman who had gone away. Every day, the lady sat underneath a drooping willow tree and cried. Her teardrops, and the leaves of the willow tree, fell into the river, where they mingled together and flowed towards the sea. Stella frowned at the poem. It was very long and dull, and impossible to learn, and surely it was quite pointless anyway, to just sit and cry into a river. If the lady wanted to find the gentleman so much, why did she not stop crying and go and look for him?

She read the first verse of the poem again and tried to commit it to memory, without success.

Preparation dragged on and on. At last, the dressing bell rang, and they all closed their books and put them away in their desks, stood up, curtsied, and filed upstairs to wash and change for supper.

'I hope she's all right,' whispered Stella to Agapanthus, as they climbed the stairs to the dormitory.

'Of course she is,' said Agapanthus, frowning.

But when they reached the dormitory, Ottilie's bed was empty. Her blankets and sheets were folded up. The drawers of her dressing table were open, and the dormitory maid was packing her trunk.

Ottilie was gone.

Six

'Where is she?' gasped Stella. 'What happened?'
The maid looked over her shoulder, and
then whispered, 'Her uncle sent for her, so he did.'

'Her uncle?' repeated Agapanthus.

'He sent some men for her,' said the maid.
'I answered the door to them. Two of them, and one
more waiting outside. The little girl didn't want to go
with them. She was up here in the dormitory, packing
a little case, and all the time she was crying. She didn't
know them, she said. She didn't want to go with
them. Fair broke my heart. But then she went into
Miss Garnet's parlour, and when she came out again,
she was as good as gold, so she was, and off she went
with them, quiet as a mouse.'

'Poor Ottilie,' said Stella.

The maid shrugged cheerfully. She slammed the
lid of the trunk and gave it a pat. 'There, that's done.

It's being called for after supper.' She picked up the folded sheets and blanket. 'It's my evening off and my young man's taking me to the Steam Fair, so he is. We'll be going on the flying boats. And the merry-go-round. And there's fireworks, later.' She giggled and went away.

At supper, Stella and Agapanthus sat beside Ottilie's empty place and ate in silence. Stella found it difficult to swallow, the dry bread stuck in her throat. She gulped a mouthful of water.

After supper, there was mending for an hour. Stella hated mending. She darned a little hole in the heel of her stocking, while Miss Mangan read another chapter of a dreary serial story from *The Young Ladies' Magazine and Moral Instructor*. It was an extremely long, annoying story called 'Florence in Fairyland', about a little girl who was stolen away from her family by a bunch of elves because they admired her golden hair and blue eyes and her pretty ways. The elves took her down to fairyland, where she went to parties, drank flower nectar and danced with fairies and goblins and mice and birds and other wild creatures, and made eyes at a handsome fairy prince.

Stella stabbed her needle into her stocking. She disliked Florence intensely, and the more she heard about her, the more she disliked her. She glanced up, frowning, and met Agapanthus's gaze. Agapanthus rolled her eyes and made a mocking, simpering face, and Stella had to bite her lip to stop herself from giggling.

The bedtime bell rang at last, and they stood up, sang the school song again, curtsied and filed up the back stairs. As they passed the door to Miss Garnet's parlour, they heard voices coming from the entrance hall. Stella twitched Agapanthus's sleeve, and they tiptoed along the passageway and peered down through the bannisters to see what was happening. Two men were carrying Ottilie's trunk through the front door. Outside, the wheels of a waiting wagon gleamed red and yellow in the light of the street lamp. The men loaded the trunk onto the wagon, and the maid closed the door behind them.

Stella and Agapanthus trailed sadly up to the dormitory. As they were undressing for bed, Stella remembered something.

'Ottilie never said anything about an uncle, did she? Just her and her mother, nobody else. And when her mother died, she was all alone. That's what she said.'

'Perhaps she didn't know about him,' whispered Agapanthus, as she pulled on her nightgown over her head. 'And perhaps her uncle heard that her mother had died and found out where she was, so he sent for her.'

'Perhaps,' said Stella doubtfully.

But it was true that sometimes people had relations they did not know about. Stella had never heard of her cousins until she had been sent away to live with them, and she had been very happy at Wormwood Mire.

She hoped Ottilie was happy. Perhaps right now she was eating a hot supper, or was already tucked up in bed at her uncle's house, sleeping peacefully.

'I hope she is all right,' she whispered.

'She's better off with her uncle, isn't she?' said Agapanthus decisively. 'Better than being here.'

That night, Stella had another frightening dream. The pale creature was chasing her again, diving through the darkness. She ran as fast as she could, gasping for breath, but the creature was faster. It caught her, clasping her around her neck with its long, clammy fingers. She was pulled off her feet, into the air. She struggled and fought, but it was too strong, and she could not escape. Its fingers were as cold as ice, and its claws dug into her neck, tearing her skin.

Suddenly, a huge owl swooped down from the sky. The creature howled. It released Stella, and she fell to the ground. The creature leaped towards the bird. The owl dived. They came together with a clash and a scream. Stella held her breath as they struggled overhead, a blur of movement in the darkness, talons raking through the air, pale fingers clawing and scratching. There was a horrible, rending sound and a shriek.

The owl fell to the ground and lay still.

'No!' gasped Stella, her voice choking. 'Gram! No!'

'No crying,' the owl whispered, right into her ear. 'No crying.'

Stella woke up, gasping for air, shaking with sobs. The dormitory was quiet. Moonlight shone in through the window, a gleaming, misty light.

She sat up and hugged her arms tightly around her knees. She could still see the owl, lying so still. Mrs Spindleweed had been hurt. Badly hurt.

'Luna,' she whispered.

There was no answer.

Stella swallowed and wiped the tears from her face, then rubbed her neck, where the creature had grabbed her. She could feel the scratches on her skin, fading as she touched them.

'Luna,' she whispered again, her voice shaking.

She remembered the musical box. It was always comforting to hold it. She listened, in case Miss McCragg was clumping around nearby, but everything was silent and still. Cautiously, she climbed out of bed, tiptoed to the door and looked out. Nothing moved.

She crept along to the washroom, slipped inside the last stall and locked the door behind her. She pulled up the linoleum and lifted the floorboard, feeling around inside the cavity. Ottilie's toy rabbit was gone, but the musical box was there. Stella clutched it and curled up on the floor. She stroked its smooth wood with shaking fingers. Her mother's name, Patience, curved across the lid in silver letters, faintly gleaming in the darkness. A tiny silver star and a moon were hidden amongst the curling pattern of flowers and leaves that decorated the box.

Stella would have loved to wind up the musical box and listen to the tinkling tune, which reminded her of Luna singing. She hummed under her breath as the tears trickled down her cheeks.

She opened the musical box. Inside was a wooden doll, a little photograph, a strip of paper with a message on it and an owl feather. She took out the photograph. It was too dark to see the picture, but that didn't matter, because she knew it by heart. Her mother, and herself and Luna, as tiny babies.

Stella picked up the owl feather and stroked it. She remembered Mrs Spindleweed saying, *I've kept her safe, all this time. And I will now.*

Stella had kept the promise she had given to Mrs Spindleweed. She had told nobody about her sister.

And now Mrs Spindleweed had tried to save Luna, and she had been hurt.

'I'm sorry,' Stella whispered to Luna in the darkness. 'Is Mrs Spindleweed all right? Are you safe?'

Stella wished there was something she could do. But there was nothing.

She touched the little doll, and then picked up the strip of paper with the message written on it. *Crossroads. Midnight. I will wait.* When they were little, her mother had taken Stella and Luna, and had gone to meet the writer of the note. But that night, their mother had died.

Stella ran her fingers along the paper. Had her father written it? Had he waited for them, at the crossroads, at midnight?

She knew nothing about her father. She did not even know his name. Who was he? And where was he? Was it from their father that she and Luna had inherited their strange ability to disappear? There was so much she didn't know.

65

Her mother was dead, but perhaps her father was still alive.

She would love to find out.

Stella put all the things carefully back inside the musical box and closed the lid. She held the box again, for a moment, and then put it back into its hiding place. As she did, her fingers brushed against something. She felt around inside the cavity and found a folded piece of paper.

She unfolded it, but it was too dark to see properly. She unlocked the door of the lavatory and tiptoed to the window, where a faint beam of moonlight slanted in. She tilted the paper into the light. It was Ottilie's tiny drawing of the fat walrus. It had been roughly torn from her sketchbook. Two words had been scribbled across the drawing. The words were shaky, but the pencil had been pressed so hard that in several places, it had made holes in the paper.

HELP ME.

Stella caught her breath.

Something touched her shoulder. She jumped and spun around. A pale figure was standing right beside her. She almost shrieked.

Agapanthus put a hand over Stella's mouth. '*Shhh.* It's only me. I couldn't sleep,' she whispered. 'I saw you were gone. What are you doing?'

Stella passed her the note. 'It's from Ottilie,' she said.

Agapanthus held the paper in the moonlight and read it. '*HELP ME*. That's her walrus. Where did you find it?'

Stella showed her the hiding place behind the lavatory. 'Something has happened to her,' she whispered.

Agapanthus turned the paper over. There was nothing on the back. 'Why didn't she write more?'

'She must have been in a hurry,' said Stella. 'She was frightened, wasn't she? I thought she was just frightened to be here at school. But perhaps there was —' She broke off and clutched Agapanthus's arm. They both heard it at the same time. Clumping footsteps.

'Quick!' whispered Stella. She pushed Agapanthus towards the door. 'Run. I'll say I had to —' She waved her hand at the lavatory.

Agapanthus hesitated, then pulled a face and darted away.

Stella dashed back into the lavatory and locked the door. The footsteps came into the washroom. Candlelight gleamed.

'Who is in there?' Miss McCragg banged on the door.

'Just me, Miss McCragg,' said Stella, trying to keep her voice steady. Had Agapanthus got back to the dormitory safely? She crouched on the floor, replacing the note in the hole, trying not to let the paper rustle. 'Stella,' she said, as she lowered the floorboard as silently as she could. 'Stella Montgomery.'

'Who is in there with you?' asked Miss McCragg.

'Nobody, Miss McCragg. It's just me.' Stella pushed the linoleum back in place and felt around in the darkness to make sure she had not missed anything. She stood up and pulled the chain of the lavatory. Taking a breath, she unlocked the door and opened it, blinking in the light of the candle.

Miss McCragg looked suspicious. 'I heard voices. Who were you talking to?'

'I was —' Stella hesitated. Then she put her hand on her middle. 'I had to use the lavatory.'

'Are you unwell?' Miss McCragg put her large hand on Stella's forehead. 'Clammy,' she said, frowning. 'Come with me. I'll give you a dose. Cod-liver oil and brimstone.'

Stella sighed. 'Yes, Miss McCragg.'

Later, lying in bed in the dark, looking up at the ceiling, with her throat burning and her mouth tasting unpleasantly of oily fish and sulphur, Stella thought of something. 'Are you awake?' she whispered.

'Yes, of course,' said Agapanthus.

Stella said, 'Yesterday, in the town, when we were walking along the High Street, we passed that man. He was pasting up posters. Ottilie was frightened. Do you remember?'

'No.'

'She was,' said Stella. She rolled over and stared at Agapanthus in the darkness. 'I'm sure she was. That man was watching her, and she was scared. We need to get a look at those posters.'

Seven

The next day, the morning lessons dragged on and on. They seemed even more tedious than usual. Stella looked at Ottilie's empty desk and thought about her note. *HELP ME*. She imagined Ottilie scribbling the words, trembling with fear. What had happened to her?

She was scolded for inattention and laziness, and Agapanthus was scolded for sulking and frowning. Dinner was boiled liver and turnips, and mutton-fat pudding, eaten in silence from new, plain plates and bowls. The weather was cloudy and overcast, but it was not raining, and so after dinner, the school set out to sketch the plants in the Wakestone Municipal Gardens.

'We need to find that poster,' whispered Stella to Agapanthus in the cloakroom, as they pulled on their boots and coats and gloves and hats.

'Yes. And I've got a good distraction for Miss Mangan,' said Agapanthus. She shot a glance over her shoulder, and then pulled her hand out of the pocket of her coat and showed Stella a dead wasp. 'I found this.' She grinned.

Stella eyed the wasp dubiously. 'How does that help?'

'Wait and see,' said Agapanthus, as she dropped the wasp back into her pocket. 'Don't worry. I'll do a distraction. And you get a look at the poster.'

As they walked along the street into the town, Stella spied the stripy cat again, running along the top of a high garden wall. He reached the end of the wall and sat there, with his tail curled around his feet, watching them pass below. He miaowed loudly and blinked his green eyes at her. She smiled and gave him a little wave, and Miss Mangan, who was walking just behind, rapped her with her umbrella.

'Eyes down,' she snapped.

They walked along the High Street. There were posters on all the lamp-posts and on the hoardings at the front of some of the shops. There were many different ones, pasted one on top of another. There were posters for tea and soap, and for false teeth and corsets, and for Steadfast Moustache Wax and Invigorating Nerve Tonic. There were several posters for missing people.

Young Female.
Missing or Taken.
Last seen in the vicinity of Crookback Court.

Stella tried to look at the posters without
moving her head too much and attracting
Miss Mangan's attention.

Reward offered to any Person
for information concerning the whereabouts of
Sir Digby Stickleback.

At last, on a lamp-post outside an elegant
hat shop with a window full of velvet ribbons
and peacock feathers and glittering beads, she
spied a poster with a galloping horse at the
top. She twitched Agapanthus's coat sleeve
and jerked her head towards the lamp-
post. Agapanthus glanced quickly over her
shoulder at Miss Mangan, and then abruptly
stopped walking and gave a piercing squeal.

Stella jumped.

Miss Mangan gasped.

Agapanthus squealed again, even more
loudly, and began to hop up and down,
flapping her arms.

'Stop that at once!' said Miss Mangan.

Agapanthus shrieked.

'Stop it!' shouted Miss Mangan. 'Whatever are you doing? Stop it at once!'

Two elderly ladies came out from the hat shop and nearly collided with Agapanthus. Their maid dropped the hat boxes she was carrying, and the hats tumbled out onto the pavement. The ladies made shrill twitters of surprise. An old gentleman nearly tripped over them and grunted in an annoyed manner. Flustered, Miss Mangan tried to step around the gentleman, apologise to the ladies and grab hold of Agapanthus all at the same time. Unnoticed, Stella sidled towards the lamp-post.

Underneath the picture of the horse was printed in big letters: *STEAM FAIR*. Stella glanced over her shoulder. A small interested crowd was gathering. Agapanthus was squealing and wriggling. Several people were scuttling around like crabs, trying to save the fallen hats from being trampled underfoot. Miss Feldspar and the other mistresses were attempting to keep the rest of the schoolgirls in line.

There was no time to read the poster. As quickly as she could, Stella tore it off the lamp-post. It was damp from the rain, but she managed to get it off in one piece. She folded it up until it was small enough to shove into her coat pocket. Then she hurried back to Agapanthus, who gave a final gasping yell and dropped a tiny object on the pavement.

'I'm sorry!' she said, panting. 'I'm so sorry, Miss Mangan. It was a wasp.'

'A wasp!' Miss Mangan repeated, her voice rising to a squeak. She poked the dead wasp with the point of her rolled-up umbrella.

'In my petticoat,' said Agapanthus. 'It was biting my —'

'Silence!' Miss Mangan smacked Agapanthus on the head with her umbrella.

'I'm sorry, Miss Mangan.'

'Such an unmannerly spectacle! Such a commotion! And in the middle of the High Street.'

'Yes, Miss Mangan. I'm very sorry, Miss Mangan,' said Agapanthus, looking contrite.

'A gentlewoman never indulges in emotional outbursts,' said Miss Mangan. 'Under any circumstances.'

'Yes, Miss Mangan,' agreed Agapanthus.

Miss Mangan gripped her arm, gave her a brisk, hard shake, said, 'Come!' and dragged her along the street to rejoin the rest of the school. Stella trotted behind them.

As they filed through the turnstiles into the

Wakestone Municipal Gardens, Agapanthus gave Stella a questioning look.

She nodded. 'I got it,' she whispered.

Agapanthus grinned.

'Begin work,' called Miss Feldspar, clapping her hands. 'In silence, if you please.'

Stella and Agapanthus walked decorously side by side across the wide lawn and followed a winding brick path into the herbaceous border, an area of ornamental iron railings and scraggly wintry shrubs.

Stella glanced behind to make sure that none of the mistresses were looking their way. 'Come on,' she whispered. They crouched down and pushed their way through the shrubs, ducking under prickly branches and dripping, wet leaves. They came out beside a row of glasshouses, tiptoed past wheelbarrows and flowerpots, and found themselves in a concealed corner of the garden, beside a large rubbish heap. There was nobody in sight.

Stella pulled the poster from her pocket. 'That was a very good distraction.'

'I know,' said Agapanthus. 'I thought Miss Mangan was going to absolutely have a spasm.' In an outraged, squeaky voice, she said, 'Stop it! Stop it at once!'

Stella giggled. She unfolded the poster, and they read it together.

STEAM FAIR

Swing Boats, Whirly-Gigs

HELTER-SKELTER

Steam-Operated Merry-Go-Round

TRY YOUR LUCK

STEAM FAIR

Sideshows, Hoop-La, Shooting Gallery

AMUSEMENTS *and Novelties*
Every evening until MIDNIGHT

FIREWORKS

Wakestone Fairground
STEAM FAIR

They read the poster again, and Agapanthus pulled a face. 'Well. It's a fair. That's nothing for Ottilie to be frightened about, is it?'

'No,' whispered Stella. She bit her lip. 'I don't know. I'm sure she saw something that scared her.'

'Miss Mangan will never let us go to a fair,' said Agapanthus. 'Of course not.'

Stella nodded. She remembered Ottilie's message. *HELP ME.* She imagined Ottilie trembling as she wrote the words. She swallowed. 'This is our only clue. We have to try, don't you think?'

Agapanthus frowned doubtfully at the poster. 'Wakestone Fairground. Where is that?'

'I don't know. We'll have to ask someone,' said Stella. 'If we're quick, perhaps we could even go and look, and get back before anyone notices that we're gone.'

Agapanthus said, 'If we are caught, we'll be in so much trouble.'

Stella nodded again. 'More trouble than if they found out about the cat and the sausages. Much more trouble.'

'So we won't get caught,' said Agapanthus decisively. 'Yes. You're right. We should try. And we should go now.'

Stella read the poster once more, then folded it up and pushed it back into her pocket. 'Come on, then,' she said. She was quite surprised to find that her voice was not shaking at all, because her insides felt extremely nervous.

They peered out from the corner of the glasshouses. There was nobody in sight. They followed a narrow path around a tangled clump of laurel bushes. The path led to the Rose Garden and, unexpectedly, they almost stumbled into Miss Mangan. She was scolding a group of Third Form girls, jabbing at their drawings with her finger. Stella and Agapanthus froze, then silently backed away as quickly as they could.

'Not that way,' said Agapanthus with a frown.

They chose another path. This one circled the duck pond. As they reached the Japanese Garden, Stella glimpsed Miss Feldspar poking disapprovingly at a plant with the point of her rolled-up umbrella. They lurked behind a clump of bamboo for several minutes, watching her through the tall stems. When her back was turned, they dashed over the arched Chinese Bridge and around behind a little pagoda and dived into a thick bank of rhododendrons. Not far away, Mlle Roche, the French mistress, was inspecting a Fourth Form girl's sketchbook in a critical manner. Stella glanced at Agapanthus, nodded and whispered, 'Go!' They sprinted through the fernery to reach the statue of a large gentleman riding a horse. They crouched behind the statue and peered cautiously out from around the horse's legs.

Across the lawn, they could see the turnstiles and the gate. They would have to be very fast, because they would be sure to be seen if any of the mistresses turned their heads. Stella took a breath. She looked at Agapanthus, who nodded.

'Now,' whispered Stella, and they darted out from behind the statue and sprinted across the grass. They barged straight through the turnstiles and out into Museum Square.

Behind them, someone shouted.

Stella hesitated.

'Come on,' said Agapanthus, grabbing Stella's hand and pulling her across the square and behind the Memorial Fountain.

Stella looked back over her shoulder and took a breath. Her heart was thumping. 'We should take the ribbons off our hats.' She pulled off the nasty, recognisable purple ribbon and pushed it into her coat pocket. Agapanthus did the same. Without the hat ribbons, they did not look like Wakestone Hall girls. They might have been anyone.

'Now, which way?' asked Stella, looking out from behind the fountain.

They asked a woman selling apples on a corner, and she pointed with a crooked finger. 'The fairground, is it? On top of Wakestone Hill. Around the museum, along Lantern Street, turn right at the end, and up the hill, my lovelies. You'll hear it before you see it, so you will.'

They ran along the street the woman had indicated, behind the museum, a cobbled laneway of little shops selling old books and coins and fossils.

Whilst in a Public Thoroughfare, every girl shall Proceed at a Restrained Velocity.

Stella felt the hard cobblestones under her feet and the cold wind whipping past her face. She grinned. Agapanthus let out a snort of laughter.

They reached the end of the street, turned right and began to climb the hill. Winding alleys snaked between the crowded houses. Tiny shops sold vegetables and fish, or boots and rope.

Stella paused to take a breath, looking back to see Museum Square down below and the town stretching out beyond, a jumble of slate roofs and grey chimneys and church towers.

They went on, weaving in and out of the people, past a public house and a group of ragged children who were playing with a spinning top. Snatches of tinny, jangling music drifted on the breeze.

'There it is,' said Agapanthus, pointing.

It was right at the top of the hill. The merry-go-round was turning, glinting in the pale sunshine.

As they got closer, they could hear the steam engines thumping and thundering. Several organs were playing different tunes. Cymbals and drums clashed together. A whistle shrieked. People shouted and hooted with laughter. Dogs barked.

They passed underneath an archway and into the fairground.

Eight

They pushed their way into the crowd. Sawdust had been sprinkled around to make the ground less slippery, but still their feet sank into the mud. The air smelled of smoke and burnt sugar.

'Ups and Downs,' bellowed a man. 'Steam-powered! Penny a ride!'

'Apple rough!' shouted a woman. 'Hot and hot. Ha'penny a cup.'

'Oranges! Sweet oranges!'

'Cobnuts!'

'Hard-bake!'

The merry-go-round was whirling in a blur of colour and jangling music. Horses and rabbits and dragons and griffons leaped and lurched, sparkling with little bits of looking glass and coloured jewels. The riders screamed.

'Ride the gallopers!' shouted a man. He saw them watching and gave them a wink. 'Penny a ride, young ladies.'

'I wish I had a penny,' said Agapanthus.

Beyond the merry-go-round was the Helter-Skelter. It was as tall as a lighthouse, painted in red and blue and gold. The polished wooden slide curled around it like a snake. There was a crowd of boys standing around the entrance, looking up. A young man appeared right at the top of the tower. Stella caught her breath as he snatched up a hessian sack and flung himself down the slide. He shrieked as he hurtled down. At the bottom, he hit the ground with a thump and tumbled over and over. His friends helped him up, laughing and patting him on the back.

'Where do we start?' asked Stella.

'We should look everywhere, and as quick as we can,' said Agapanthus firmly. 'Come on.'

They made their way through the fairground, past the rides and sideshows. The swing boats swooped by overhead. There were advertisements for a Bearded Lady (*ASTONISHING SPECTACLE*), a Giant (*ALWAYS ON SHOW, ALIVE*) and a group of Mechanical Dancers (*DIVERTING* and *INGENIOUS*). Cheers and shouts came from inside the tents. There were stalls selling toffee apples, paper pinwheels and tin trumpets, and gilded gingerbread in the shapes of horses and hearts and crowns. A group of children dashed by, blowing whistles and screeching.

'Try your luck!' shouted a man. He held a handful of coloured wooden balls. In the stall behind him was a row of grinning clown dolls with staring, round eyes and mops of woolly hair. 'Try your luck, young ladies. Knock down a dolly and win a prize. Penny a throw.'

They hurried on, passing a Hoop-La and a cocoanut shy and a fishing game, with prizes of goldfish in glass jars.

There was no sign of Ottilie anywhere.

At a shooting gallery, men were firing rifles at a row of metal ducks that jerked along a track. *Crack! Crack! Crack!* There was a smell of burnt gunpowder.

Stella heard a muffled yell and stopped. In a narrow alley between the fishing game and the shooting gallery, two heavily built men were standing over a ragged, barefoot boy. The men wore leather waistcoats and bowler hats, and coloured handkerchiefs around

their necks. One of them was chewing on a chop, gravy dripping down his chin.

The boy was clutching a wooden tray of tiny glittering flowers. His arms were wrapped around it protectively.

One of the men pushed the boy, making him stumble backwards. 'Go on. Git.' He shoved him harder and the boy fell, landing in the mud with a thump. The contents of his tray scattered.

'Git on with you,' said the second man. He gave the fallen boy a kick.

The first man said, 'And if we see you here again, it'll be worse for you.' He stamped on the fallen flowers with the heel of his boot, grinding them into the mud. The other man spat before they turned and walked away.

The boy sat up, groaning. He was pale and thin. His hair was the colour of straw and stuck out in wisps from under his shabby cap. His knee was bleeding. He touched it gingerly, and then wiped his eyes with the back of his muddy sleeve. Stella went over to him and crouched down. She took out her handkerchief and dabbed at the blood as gently as she could, then tied the handkerchief around his knee.

Agapanthus fished in the top of her stocking and handed him a toffee. 'Here,' she said, patting his shoulder.

'Thank you,' he said. He unwrapped the silver paper and put the toffee in his mouth.

'Are you all right?' asked Stella. 'Can you walk?'

They helped him to his feet.

'Likely,' said the boy, taking a tentative, limping step. He nodded, then bent down gingerly and began to collect the fallen flowers. Stella and Agapanthus helped him. The flowers were tiny and delicate, made from wire and glass beads. Stella collected a daisy and a buttercup and a forget-me-not. They had been stamped into the mud, squashed and broken.

'Who were those men?' asked Agapanthus, as she passed the boy a dandelion and a cornflower.

'Them? The Gabbro brothers.' The boy sucked the toffee and shrugged. 'There's three of 'em. They're hired by the fairground for keepin' order. No flats on the tober, that's what they say.' He glanced up, saw their confused faces and explained, 'It means no hawkin' on the fairground. I din't see them comin' up behind me, that time. I got to be a good bit nippier and keep a leery eye out, so I do.'

Stella picked up a bluebell and passed it to him. 'These are very pretty,' she said.

He nodded. 'Tuppence each,' he said hopefully. 'Four a tanner.'

'I'm sorry,' said Stella, as she handed him a violet. 'We don't have any money. Did you make them?'

'My sister.' The boy carefully bent the muddy violet back into shape, spat on it and rubbed it clean on the front of his ragged shirt. The tiny glass beads sparkled. He laid it carefully beside the others on the tray. He looked around. 'That's the lot,' he said, and stood up. 'I'm Joe.'

'I'm Stella,' said Stella.

'Agapanthus,' said Agapanthus.

'That's a name and a half, ain't it?' Joe grinned. 'Well. I'm right obliged to you, so I am. And you'll be wanting your wiper back.' He bent down to untie Stella's handkerchief from his knee.

'Please keep it. Are you sure you're all right?' asked Stella doubtfully.

He gave another grin and a little jerk of his head. 'I'm prime,' he said, and then limped away, disappearing into the crowd.

Stella and Agapanthus watched him go.

'Come on,' said Agapanthus. 'If we don't get back soon, we'll be in so much trouble. We have to hurry.'

At the edge of the fairground they came to a stretch of open, muddy ground. Tethered horses were cropping the grass, between wagons and carts, and piles of timber and canvas.

Stella spied a shabby-looking wagon with red-and-yellow wheels. She grabbed Agapanthus's arm. 'That's the wagon that came and collected Ottilie's trunk, isn't it?' she said.

'I don't know. Is it?' Agapanthus frowned.

'I think so. It had red-and-yellow wheels, just like these,' said Stella. She looked around, to make sure that nobody was watching them, and tried the door of the wagon, but it was locked with a heavy iron padlock.

From inside came a faint scrabbling sound.

'Did you hear something?' Stella asked.

Agapanthus shook her head.

There was a little dusty window. Stella jumped, but it was too high and she could not see in.

Agapanthus bent down. 'Climb up on my back,' she said. Stella clambered up, and Agapanthus stood, wobbling. Stella clutched the windowsill. '

'Steady,' she said, trying to peer inside.

Agapanthus wobbled again, her feet slipping. 'Oops!' she gasped, then lost her balance and collapsed. They both fell sprawling into the mud.

Agapanthus helped Stella up. 'I am sorry,' she said. She picked up her hat and crammed it back onto her head. 'Did you see anything?'

'No, it was too dark inside.' Stella rubbed her elbow and inspected a large hole in her stocking.

'Miss Mangan won't like this, will she?' she said, grinning ruefully as she tried to brush the wet mud from her skirt.

'She will utterly explode!' Agapanthus gave a snort of laughter. She spied her purple hat ribbon lying in the mud, picked it up and pushed it back into her coat pocket. 'Well. Let's try again —'

'What are you two doin' back here?'

They jumped and spun around. Three men appeared from behind the wagon. Two of them were the men who had been pushing Joe. The Gabbro brothers. All three looked very alike, broad-shouldered and thickset.

'N-nothing,' stammered Stella.

'It ain't safe for little morts round here.' The first brother frowned. 'In particklar, pryin' little morts who poke their noses where they ain't wanted.'

The second brother nodded and rubbed his hands together. His knuckles cracked.

The third brother finished the chop he was gnawing on, threw away the bone and wiped the gravy off his face with the back of his hand.

Stella and Agapanthus stepped backwards.

'W-we aren't doing anything,' said Stella.

'Git on your way, then,' said the first one. He jerked his thumb back towards the fairground. 'Go on. Git.'

Stella grabbed Agapanthus's arm. 'We're just going,' she said, and they turned and hurried away. Stella looked back and saw the three brothers were standing beside the red-and-yellow wagon, watching them go. One of them said something, and the other two laughed.

'The Gabbro brothers,' said Agapanthus.

Stella nodded. 'It was one of them that was pasting up those posters yesterday. I'm sure. That's what frightened Ottilie, I think. She saw him, and it frightened her.' She looked back over her shoulder and caught her breath.

One of the brothers was following them.

'Come on.' They went a bit faster. They passed the sideshows and skirted the swing boats, pushing their way through the crowd. A whistle shrieked, making Stella's heart thump. They went along as quickly as they could, their feet slipping on the muddy ground. Someone stepped backwards, thumping into Stella, and she nearly fell over.

The man following them shouted something, and the man on the Hoop-La shouted back and laughed.

The music from the steam organs jangled. The engines thundered and shrieked. Inside a tent, someone screamed with laughter.

Stella glanced behind. The man was getting closer.

'This way. Quick.' Agapanthus grabbed Stella's hand and dragged her into a narrow alley beside the cocoa-nut shy, pulling her down behind a sack of cocoa-nuts. They crouched there and watched the man pass. He was walking quickly, frowning, scanning the crowd.

They made their way cautiously between the tents and stalls, sliding through narrow gaps, ducking under ropes. They emerged from around the side of a gingerbread stall, not far from the merry-go-round.

'I think we lost him,' said Agapanthus.

Before Stella could answer, someone grabbed her arm. She gasped in shock as she was pulled off her feet and spun around.

A dark shape loomed above her. Stella shrieked.

It was Miss Mangan.

Nine

The mistress towered over them, her black cloak flapping in the breeze. Her face was like thunder.

'Outrageous,' she hissed. 'Shocking. Deplorable.'

Stella gasped. 'M-Miss Mangan. We were looking for Ott—'

'Silence!' Miss Mangan gave Stella a shake that made her teeth bang together and her ears ring.

'But —' Stella tried to explain. 'She was —'

Miss Mangan shook her again, until Stella was too dizzy to think. 'Not one word,' she snapped. 'Not one. You should both be ashamed of yourselves. You are in utter disgrace. Come with me.'

She dragged them back to the entrance of the fairground, gripping their arms tightly as she strode along. She walked so fast that they had to jog to keep up with her.

Stella looked across at Agapanthus, and Agapanthus rolled her eyes and grimaced. Miss Mangan did not notice and did not slow down. She marched them out of the fairground and down the hill, and then along the High Street, past all the grand shops. It began to drizzle, and she did not stop to open her umbrella, which she carried hooked over her arm, but strode along through the rain, her breath coming in angry hisses.

By the time they reached the school, Stella was wet through and out of breath. Miss Mangan pulled them up the stairs and into the cloakroom, where she gave them one last shake and released her grip at last. Stella rubbed her bruised arm, and once more she tried to explain.

'I'm sorry, Miss Mangan,' she started to say. 'We were looking for Ottilie. She was —'

'Silence!' said Miss Mangan. 'I will not listen to any of your excuses. A fairground! The thought of it! Look at your stockings! Appalling. And where are your hat ribbons?'

Stella fished into the pocket of her wet coat and pulled out the hat ribbon. She untangled it and put it back on her hat, as well as she could with trembling fingers. She hung her hat on its hook. Agapanthus was slow to untangle her hat ribbon, and Miss Mangan slapped her.

'Foolish girls,' she said. 'Foolish, wilful, thoughtless girls. Anything could have happened to you.' She took an angry breath and added, 'As soon as you have made yourselves presentable, Miss Garnet will see you in her parlour. Certainly, once she has done with you, there will be no more of this behaviour. You mark my words.'

Stella shivered. She did not know what happened inside Miss Garnet's parlour, and she did not want to find out. She pulled off her wet gloves and coat and sat down to unlace her boots. Her fingers were still shaking.

Miss Mangan led them up to the dormitory and stood over them as they brushed their hair and plaited it. She dipped a rough flannel into a jug of icy water and rubbed it over their faces, making them gasp for breath.

When they were ready, Miss Mangan looked them up and down, nodded, said, 'Follow me,' and marched them down the stairs to the door of Miss Garnet's parlour. 'Stand there.' She pointed.

They stood side by side against the wall. Stella looked down at her shoes. She did not dare to risk even one glance at Agapanthus. She swallowed. She was determined not to cry.

Miss Mangan knocked on the door of the parlour. Miss Garnet's grim-faced maid appeared. 'Yes, Madam?'

Miss Mangan stepped inside, and the maid closed the door behind her.

Stella took a shaking breath and whispered quickly, 'I'm so sorry. I thought we might find Ottilie at the fairground. I really did. And now we're in dreadful trouble, and it's my fault. It was all for nothing.'

'But she was there,' whispered Agapanthus. 'Look.' With her eyes on the parlour door, she quickly pulled something out of the sleeve of her dress and passed it to Stella. It was a muddy hat ribbon. Sewn in tiny stitches was a name. *Ottilie Smith.*

'Ottilie's ribbon!'

'Yes. It was near that wagon where we fell over. I thought it was mine. I picked it up and shoved it in my pocket. But when we got back here, I had two of them. My one, and this one too. She must have dropped it.'

'So, she was there,' breathed Stella. 'Perhaps she was in the wagon all the time.'

'Yes. We have to go back.'

Stella nodded, winding the hat ribbon around her fingers. Agapanthus was right. They had to go back and rescue Ottilie, if they could.

The parlour door opened, and Miss Mangan came out. Stella whipped the ribbon behind her back. Miss Mangan frowned at them and said, 'Miss Garnet will see you now.' She pointed at Agapanthus. 'You first.'

Agapanthus knocked on the parlour door. The maid opened the door, and Agapanthus went inside.

'Wait right there,' said Miss Mangan to Stella, then she turned and stalked away, up the stairs towards the classrooms.

Stella stood alone in the cold hallway, twisting Ottilie's hat ribbon between her fingers.

It was very quiet. She could hear voices from the classrooms upstairs. A carriage drove past outside. A flurry of raindrops blew against the window, and a cold breath of air snaked along the passageway. For a moment, Stella remembered the horrible pale creature from her dream, with its long, icy fingers. She shivered.

A sudden sharp cry from inside Miss Garnet's parlour made her jump. Her heart gave a lurch like a fish caught on a line. She held her breath, listening, but all she could hear was the sound of the rain. Another carriage drove past. Minutes passed.

At last, the door opened and Agapanthus came out. Her face was white and expressionless. Her freckles stood out like tiny spots of ink.

'You're to go in now,' was all she said. She did not meet Stella's eyes. She turned and walked away towards the stairs. She did not look back.

Stella hesitated, watching Agapanthus climb the

stairs. Then she pushed Ottilie's hat ribbon into her pocket, took a breath and knocked on the parlour door.

Miss Garnet's parlour was a large room and rather dark. Heavy velvet curtains hung at the windows. It was warm, and it smelled of lavender and mildew. The only sounds were the ticking of a tall grandfather clock and the fire crackling in the grate.

As Stella's eyes became accustomed to the darkness, she saw that the room was full of little tables and cabinets, and every surface was covered with ornaments. There were shelves everywhere, and they were crammed with trinkets, glimmering in the firelight. Stella gazed around at the ornaments. Nearby on a small table was a china dog decorated with painted flowers and the words *A Present from Southsea*, a green glass cat, an ivory fan, a little ship made out of beads, a basket covered with shells and a silk pincushion in the shape of a hedgehog with pearl-headed pins stuck into it. Everywhere she looked were figurines and souvenirs, pincushions and paperweights.

'Come closer,' said a voice.

Miss Garnet was sitting in an armchair near the fire, half-hidden amongst all the ornaments. She was a plump, elderly lady, with immaculate white hair and colourless, protruding eyes. Her skin was as pale as mutton fat. She wore a lace cap and a figured silk gown, decorated with tiny, gleaming beads. She was turning the pages of a large photograph album. On the table beside her were an ivory elephant, a china thimble, a vase of flowers made out of peacock feathers and a cake stand full of tiny cakes and sandwiches.

Stella swallowed nervously and tried to stop herself from shaking. She took three steps forward, careful to avoid brushing against another low table full of ornaments. She curtsied.

'Closer.'

Stella hesitated, and then took two more steps.

Miss Garnet gestured at the ornaments. 'Mementos from my girls. They remember their old Headmistress.' She smiled. 'They are all in here.' She laid her hand on the photograph album. 'All my girls. Look.'

The album contained silhouettes of girls' heads. They had been cut from black paper and glued into elaborate frames that were adorned with roses and scrolls and curling leaves. They were tiny, but extraordinarily lifelike. Miss Garnet ran her finger along the rows of faces, and then turned a page to reveal still more pictures.

'I take an image with my physiognograph of every girl in her first term at school here —' She put a spoonful of sugar into her cup of tea, stirred it and took a sip. '— as soon as a girl's character becomes clear to me, and I have identified her particular faults.' She tapped one of the pictures with the tip of her pale finger. 'This is Theodora d'Arcy. Laziness.' Miss Garnet considered the tiny image with her head on one side. In the dim, flickering firelight, the silhouette seemed almost alive. Stella blinked. She almost thought she saw Theodora turn her head, just a fraction. Miss Garnet said, 'She is Lady Cholmondeley now, of course. And just last month, she sent me this, from Alexandria.' Miss Garnet reached out to a nearby shelf and laid her finger on a shiny brass camel. 'She is rather busy there, organising the natives.' She gave the camel a little smile, took another sip of tea and turned the page.

'Here is Dorothea Hamilton.' She touched a picture. 'Dishonesty.' Her finger moved to the next face. 'Veronica St Aubrey. Vanity. Always admiring herself in the mirror, I recall. And this is Frederica

Fitzgerald. Sulkiness. I cannot abide a sulky girl. Saisha Vengalil. Despondency. That girl would have spent her whole time crying in corners, if she had been given her own way. She went on to marry the Nawab of Tonk, of course.' Miss Garnet turned several pages, running her finger over the rows of faces. 'Marguerite Cavendish. Carelessness. And here is Philadelphia Courtenay. Intemperance. Immoderation. Dissipation. I had to take her image three times, and even so, I saw insufficient improvement in her behaviour, and I was obliged to expel her.' She sighed and picked up a miniature pink cake from her tea tray and ate it in three tiny bites.

She turned page after page, murmuring to herself, until she reached the final pictures in the album. There were only two faces on the page. Miss Garnet rested her finger on Ottilie and then on Agapanthus. There were lines of tiny, silvery writing underneath, but from where Stella was standing, she could not read it. Reluctantly, she took another step closer to the Headmistress. The writing was immaculate. *Ottilie Smith. Intractability. Agapanthus Ffaulkington-Ffitch. Insubordination.*

Ottilie and Agapanthus were the last images in the album. The remaining frames on the page were empty and waiting. Miss Garnet tapped the next empty frame with the tip of her finger. She said,

'Your Aunts informed me that you are inclined to waywardness. As was your mother.' She pursed her lips with distaste.

Stella wanted very much to know about her mother. What had she done that was so dreadful? Nervously, she took a shaking breath. 'Please, M-Miss Garnet, what —?'

Miss Garnet went on as if Stella had not spoken at all, 'And now, Miss Mangan tells me that you have proved to be wilfully disobedient. I trust you are ashamed of yourself.'

'Y-yes, Miss Garnet,' said Stella.

Miss Garnet nodded. 'If you misbehave again, I will be obliged to summon your Aunts. I do not suppose you would welcome that.'

Stella swallowed. 'No, Miss Garnet.'

'You have been sent to school to correct the faults in your character. Wakestone Hall has many rules, and you must learn to obey them all.'

'Yes, Miss Garnet.'

'And when your faults have been corrected, you will find your time here at Wakestone Hall to be so very much more agreeable.'

Stella gazed down at the pictures of Ottilie and Agapanthus. In the flickering light, it was easy to believe they were somehow trapped in the tiny, shadowy images. Stella imagined she saw a wisp of Ottilie's hair move. And Agapanthus seemed to lift her chin and open her mouth as if she were about to speak.

'Now. Sit there.' Miss Garnet gestured towards an alcove. The grim-faced maid came forward from where she had been standing in the shadows and drew aside a curtain to reveal a wooden chair with an oddly shaped, high, straight back, beside a desk on which was a gleaming instrument, rather like a microscope.

Unwillingly, Stella went across to the chair, avoiding two little tables and a what-not stand crowded with ornaments, and sat down gingerly on the edge of the seat.

Miss Garnet lifted a finger, and the maid pushed Stella firmly against the back of the chair. There was a winding sound, and Stella felt something sliding upwards. A cold metal shape curved around her head. Something clicked. She reached up and touched a clamp that was gripping the back of her head. The maid passed a leather strap around her neck, pulled it tight and buckled it.

'Now, you must sit perfectly still,' said Miss Garnet.

Stella tried to nod, but could not. She could not move her head at all. So she said, 'Y-yes, Miss Garnet.' She was shaking. Her mouth was dry. She gripped the arms of the chair with her fingers.

'Perfectly still,' repeated Miss Garnet. She put the photograph album aside, stood up with a rustle of silk and moved to stand in front of Stella. She gave her a little smile. 'Do not agitate yourself. It will hardly hurt. And after it is done, you will find that you do not remember it at all.'

Ten

*M*iss Garnet gestured again, and the maid pulled several brass attachments from the sides of the chair. They extended forward and clicked into place. On one side of Stella's head she positioned a small lantern. On the other side, a transparent silk screen. Stella could only turn her eyes, so it was difficult to see exactly what was happening. She watched as the maid struck a match, lit the lantern and opened a shutter. A beam of bright light shone onto the side of Stella's face. Her shadow fell onto the screen. She blinked, and on the screen her shadow blinked as well.

Stella took a breath and tried to stop trembling.

The maid adjusted the position of the screen and the lantern, then stepped back, out of Stella's sight. Miss Garnet sat down at the desk and perched a pair of silver spectacles on the bridge of her nose. She said to Stella, 'This is the physiognograph. A rather ingenious invention. It was made for me many years ago.'

Stella looked at the instrument out of the corner of her eye. It had lenses and mirrors like a microscope, and a number of tiny wheels, like the insides of a clock. It was made of gleaming dark wood, brass and ivory.

Miss Garnet swivelled a mirror, moving it the smallest fraction of an inch, reflecting the image from the screen onto a lens. Stella saw her shadow appear upside down on a tiny mirror, and then again, right way up, on a second mirror.

Miss Garnet picked up a piece of paper. It was a list of the school rules, the same list that was pasted on the walls of all the schoolrooms and the dormitories. She mounted it carefully into a bracket at the bottom of the instrument and swivelled it into place.

'The physiognograph captures images, of course,' she said, as she peered into an eye piece and slowly turned a brass knob. 'It makes a precise copy of your shadow. And it does a little more than that. As you will see. Be sure to remain perfectly still.' She adjusted a tiny wheel.

Stella saw her shadow appear on the list of rules. It was only two inches high and very clear. She swallowed. Her tiny shadow swallowed as well.

'Very good,' said Miss Garnet. She moved a lever, and a silver knife, as sharp as a needle, descended. The point of the knife touched the paper.

Despite the warmth of the room, Stella felt an icy shiver trickle down her spine.

Miss Garnet slowly turned a brass handle, and the knife began to cut a line around the edge of the shadow.

Stella felt as if she had been pierced, near her heart, with a fine, cold needle. She cried out in pain.

'Silence, if you please,' said Miss Garnet.

Stella bit her lip and tried not to make any sound,

gripping the wooden armrests of the chair so tightly that her fingers ached.

The knife cut around her shadow. Up the back of her neck, around her wispy hair, strand by strand, then over the top of her head and down her face, forehead, nose, mouth and chin.

'Very good,' Miss Garnet said at last.

Stella took a shaky breath. Miss Garnet held up the tiny paper shape. Stella gazed at it. It looked exactly like her. She shuddered, and between Miss Garnet's white fingers the fragile image shuddered as well.

Miss Garnet dipped a fine brush into a bottle of ink and carefully painted over Stella's image, covering the lines of writing. She laid it aside to dry. She looked at Stella and said, 'Once you are in my album, you will find it easier to obey all the rules, I do assure you.'

The maid carried the photograph album from the fireside and laid it open on the desk. Miss Garnet brushed glue onto the back of the paper shape. She turned it over and stuck it carefully into the empty frame, beside the pictures of Ottilie and Agapanthus, pressing it into place very delicately with the tips of her fingers. She picked up a silver pencil. '*Stella Montgomery*,' she said as she wrote. '*Wilful Disobedience*. There. It is done.' She ran her fingers over the tiny black silhouette and closed the album.

The maid unbuckled the strap around Stella's neck. The metal clasp let go of the back of her head and retracted into the chair.

'Now, you may stand up,' said Miss Garnet.

Stella stumbled to her feet, dizzy and shaking. The bell rang. Miss Garnet looked at the clock and said, 'You have missed several lessons. French Conversation, I believe. And Household Management. You will have to work hard to ensure you do not fall behind. But now you may go and join your form for Preparation.'

Stella curtsied and walked out of the parlour. She closed the door carefully behind her and climbed the stairs to the First Form classroom. She knocked on the door, entered, curtsied to Miss Mangan, walked to her seat and sat down.

During Lessons, Girls will give their full Attention to their Work and Avoid Distractions of any Description.

Stella did not look at anyone. She opened her notebook.

She felt rather dazed, as if she had just woken up from a deep sleep. But it was time for Preparation, and so she must give her full attention to her work. She must learn the long, sad poem. Stella committed the first verse to memory, and then started to learn the second verse. The sad lady sat beside the willow tree and cried into the river.

At the end of the second verse, Stella glanced up from her book for a moment and saw that Miss Mangan was watching her with a satisfied little smile. Stella looked down again and began to learn the third verse of the poem. The lady continued to cry. The leaves continued to fall off the willow tree. They landed in the river and floated away.

Agapanthus was also studying silently. She did not look up from her book. The room was quiet. The only sounds were the clock ticking and the rain pattering against the window.

Supper was bread and water.

Girls shall Sit Correctly at the Table, and eat with Decorum and Poise.

Stella kept her elbows in and sat up as straight as she could as she ate her supper. It was important to sit correctly. Agapanthus's face had no expression at all as she decorously chewed and swallowed a piece of dry bread. She picked up her cup of water and took a sip.

After supper, they sat side by side and darned their stockings and listened to the next chapter of 'Florence in Fairyland', which Miss Mangan read to them from *The Young Ladies' Magazine and Moral Instructor*.

Stella concentrated on her sewing and did not lift her eyes from her work.

Girls shall mend all their own Clothes, and Endeavour to do so Neatly.

It was important to sew neatly. Stella worked carefully to make a neat darn. She could not think how she had come to have such a large hole in her stocking. She could not recall anything that might have caused it. Trying to remember made her feel dizzy.

She saw Miss Mangan watching her again, with the same satisfied little smile as before. Stella looked down and listened to Florence's adventures in Fairyland as she sewed carefully, making the stitches as small and neat as she could manage.

Suddenly, she had the odd feeling that someone was trying to get her attention. The voice was very faint, as if it was coming from a long way away. She looked around, blinking, but everybody was sewing silently, heads down.

'Eyes down.' Miss Mangan was frowning at her.

Stella looked down and went on sewing. It was important to sew neatly. She sewed the neatest stitches she could manage.

When the bedtime bell rang, Stella stood up and sang the school song with everyone else.

Wakestone Girls don't flinch or fail,
Marching on, we will prevail.
Duty is the hardest fight,
Always Righteous, Always Right.

Later, as she was undressing for bed in the dormitory, folding her clothes carefully and putting them away in her drawers, she had the strange feeling again. As if someone was calling her name.

Stella.

The voice seemed to appear in her mind like a flickering candle flame.

Stella looked around, but everyone was getting undressed in silence. Agapanthus was unbuttoning her dress. Stella did the same. She shook out her dress carefully and went to hang it up in the wardrobe.

She must have imagined the voice, because it was against the rules to speak to another girl in the dormitory, and it was very important to obey the rules.

If she heard the voice again, she would certainly ignore it.

She picked up her hairbrush.

Girls Shall brush their Hair twice every day, Morning and Night, counting two hundred strokes.

Stella ignored the voice in her head as she brushed her hair and carefully counted to two hundred.

Eleven

*T*hat night, Stella had another dream. A voice whispered into her ear. A tiny voice, faint but clear.

Get up.

In her dream, Stella sat up in bed. It was cold. Somewhere far away, a clock was striking. Stella counted the chimes. Ten o'clock.

She listened for a moment. There was nothing to hear but the rain on the roof and music playing, somewhere far away. A tinkling, melancholy tune.

Get up.

Without meaning to do it, Stella climbed out of the bed. She tiptoed along the room to the doorway at the end and looked out into the passageway. It was dark.

Fade, said the voice, and Stella felt herself disappear, vanishing into the shadows as easily as blinking.

Go on.

She crept along the passageway, as silent as a mouse, as invisible as a breath of wind. She hesitated at the top of a staircase, but the voice was insistent, and so she tiptoed down. Under her breath, she sang along to the distant, tinkling music. On the floor below that, there were lights under some of the doors, and she could hear voices murmuring within the rooms. Stella crept silently past and went on, down the next flight of stairs.

She came to another passageway and followed it until she reached a door. It was closed. She hesitated.

Listen.

Stella crept closer and put her ear against the door. There was nothing to hear. She touched the door handle with her invisible fingers. She did not know what was inside the room. She did not want to open the door.

Go on.

She turned the handle as silently as she could, pushed the door open and slipped inside. She closed the door softly behind her.

She was in Miss Garnet's parlour. It was lit with candles. A fire flickered in the grate. Her eye fell on a glass frog, a silver giraffe, a little jug with a picture of a waterfall on it, a beaded goldfish with scales made of sequins. Everywhere she looked, trinkets and ornaments glinted in the candlelight.

Her gaze fell on the album, on a chair beside the fireplace.

That's it, said the voice. *Open it.*

Stella picked up the book, sat down and began to turn the pages, looking at the rows of tiny faces. Some of them were still, but some seemed to flicker and twitch in the candlelight. She turned page after page, until she reached the last pictures in the book. There were three faces in a row. After those three pictures, the frames were empty.

Burn it.

Stella carefully tore the page from the book, took it to the fireplace and threw it on the flames.

She picked up the poker and pushed the page into the heart of the fire.

Stella woke up with a terrifying jolt. She should have been lying in bed, but instead she was standing with a poker in her hand, watching a shower of silvery flames shooting up the chimney. She dropped the poker and nearly toppled into the fireplace.

What had happened? Where was she? She took a gasping breath and looked around the room, bewildered.

Her heart gave a sickening lurch.

Miss Garnet's parlour.

She took a step backwards. Her head was spinning, and she lost her balance and knocked a big book onto the floor. It fell open, toppling a little table. Ornaments scattered across the carpet. Stella hurriedly crouched to pick them up. Her hands were shaking. She pushed the table upright and put the ornaments back on top.

She stumbled to her feet. If she were caught here, she would be in the most dreadful trouble.

And then she remembered the insistent voice. Luna's voice. Her sister had been telling her what to do as she slept. She saw the photograph album, lying open on the floor. All at once, she remembered how Miss Garnet had made a picture of her and stuck her in the album, trapping her.

Shuddering, she picked up the album. One of the images made her catch her breath. The face had a definite, straight nose, and the hair was pulled back from a high forehead and arranged in an uncompromising, old-fashioned style.

Underneath the picture, in tiny silver letters, was written:

Deliverance Montgomery.
Wilful Disobedience.

It was the same thing that Miss Garnet had written under her own picture. As Stella watched, the young Aunt Deliverance seemed to tilt her head, almost as if she were about to say something.

More writing had been added underneath the picture.

Needlework Prize.
Etiquette Prize.
Elocution Prize.
Countess Anstruther's Correct Conduct Medal,
    Three Times.
HEAD GIRL.

Miss Garnet had turned Aunt Deliverance from a disobedient child into a prize-winning Head Girl.

Stella wondered if she should tear out the page and burn it in the fire. What would happen to Aunt Deliverance if she did?

She closed the album, and then hesitated. She listened. Everything was quiet. This might be her only chance to find out about her mother.

She sat down, opened the album again and began to search through the pages as quickly as she could.

She ran her finger along the names, turning page after page, passing rows and rows of faces. She found Aunt Temperance, *Inattention*, and a bit later, Aunt Condolence, *Self-Indulgence*.

She looked at the little faces. It was so strange to think about the Aunts as schoolgirls.

And then at last she saw it. Her mother's picture.

Patience Montgomery.
Waywardness.

A thin face, with wispy hair. Stella ran her finger over the tiny image. It did not move.

Waywardness. What did that mean, exactly?

Underneath that, in larger, more spiky writing, she read:

Wilful, Wanton, Wicked.
Run Away with an Unacceptable Person.

And underneath that, largest and spikiest of all, was written:

EXPELLED.

Stella caught her breath.

From somewhere nearby, she heard a noise. Footsteps were approaching. Stella jumped up and flung the album onto the chair. She looked around, but there was nowhere to hide. She darted into a corner beside the fireplace, took a breath, gritted her teeth and forced herself to disappear. For a moment, she thought she could not manage it, but then she felt the horrible, dizzying feeling as she faded away into the shadows.

The parlour door opened, and Miss Garnet came into the room, followed by a gentleman. He looked rather similar to her, plump and pale, with protruding eyes. He had a thick white moustache and whiskers. He carried an ebony-and-silver walking stick in one hand and held a shiny silk top hat under his arm.

Stella stood as still as a stone, hardly breathing. She could feel her heart beating in her ears.

Miss Garnet turned to him and frowned. 'Well. I have done my part, Thaddeus. At some risk to my reputation.'

The gentleman said, 'I promise you, Drusilla —' He had a smooth, oily voice.

Miss Garnet frowned. 'Promises. Fine words, brother. But you have achieved nothing.'

'On the contrary, Drusilla. I am close to success,' he said, rubbing his hands together. 'But I admit there have been unforeseen obstacles. Delays and impediments.'

'As usual, you have complicated things unnecessarily. You were like this as a child. Devious and unreliable. And with an unfortunate attraction to disreputable company.' She touched the gleaming physiognograph with the tip of her finger. 'If you were one of my girls, brother, I would correct those faults.'

He took a step away from her and said, 'Mercifully, I am not one of your unfortunate girls. I made that device for you, and I know precisely what it can do.' He pulled on his gloves and gave a bow. 'I will depart. I have an appointment. If everything goes to plan, I trust I will have better news for you tomorrow. Good evening, Drusilla, my dear.' He put on his hat.

Miss Garnet rang the bell, and when her grim-faced maid appeared, she said, 'Show my brother out.' When the maid returned a few minutes later, she added, 'Tidy this room, then bring me a cup of hot chocolate and a plate of buttered toast. Hot, mind. To my bedroom.'

'Yes, Madam.'

Miss Garnet went through a door on the other side of the room and closed it behind her. Stella watched as the maid poked at the fire and hung the poker on a hook. She picked up the album from where Stella had left it on the chair and put it away on a shelf. She straightened several of the ornaments. Then she blew out the candles and, at last, left the room too.

Stella waited a moment or two, and then let herself become visible again, which made her head swim. She was stiff from standing so still. She took a breath, crept to the door, listened, then opened it cautiously and looked out. The passageway was empty. She slipped out of the parlour, closed the door softly behind her and tiptoed back up the stairs to the dormitory, as silently as a cat.

Agapanthus was sitting up in bed. 'What happened? What did you do?' she whispered.

Stella hesitated. She could not tell Agapanthus about Luna. And it was too strange, anyway. How could she explain that she had an invisible sister who told her what to do when she was asleep? 'I think I was sleepwalking,' she said. 'And when I woke up, I was standing in the parlour, burning the page from the album with our pictures on it.'

Agapanthus whispered, 'Wasn't it utterly dreadful? It was like being stuck in a nightmare. All I could think about were all those horrible rules. Miss Garnet turned me into a good, quiet, obedient little girl.' She shuddered. 'I utterly cannot believe she could do that to me.'

'I know,' said Stella. 'It was the same for me.'

'But then I woke up. And I remembered it all. And also, I remembered that we have to go and save Ottilie. And I think that we need to go right now. Because as soon as Miss Garnet finds out what you've done, she'll put us back in the album, straight away, won't she?'

'Or maybe she'll do something worse,' said Stella.

'Yes,' agreed Agapanthus. 'And perhaps next time you won't go sleepwalking and save us. And we might be stuck like that forever. Like all the other girls here. I'd like to burn the whole album and smash that machine to bits.'

Stella looked at the shapes of the obedient sleeping girls. 'Let's go, then,' she whispered. 'This might be our only chance.'

Agapanthus climbed out of bed, and they pushed their pillows under the blankets.

'Let's get dressed in the washroom,' whispered Stella. They collected their clothes as silently as they could, bundled them up and tiptoed to the washroom. Stella struggled to get dressed in the darkness. Her fingers were cold, and she fumbled with the buttons and tapes. Agapanthus lost her balance and clutched Stella to steady herself, and they both broke into muffled giggles.

When she was ready at last, Stella went into the lavatory and felt around for the hiding place under the floorboard. She took out the little musical box and shoved it in the pocket of her dress. It was foolish, most likely, but she was so nervous, it would be comforting to have it with her.

They tiptoed down the stairs as quietly as they could. A sound made them freeze, and they ducked behind a doorway and watched as Miss McCragg clumped past, carrying a candle. They waited, holding their breath, until she went up the stairs. They crept on, past the mistresses' rooms and the classrooms, and then down the back stairs to the cloakroom. In the darkness, they felt around for their damp coats, hats and boots and pulled them on. They took off the hat ribbons and pushed them into their coat pockets.

When they were ready, Agapanthus whispered, 'Time to go.'

Light shone in through the coloured windows around the big front door. Agapanthus bent down and pulled back the bottom bolt. Stella stood on tiptoe to reach the top bolt. She shoved it across and opened the door.

The rain had stopped. Mist swirled, making the street lamps flicker.

Stella hesitated on the top step. The night was very cold, and somehow much bigger and darker than she had imagined it might be. She shivered.

Agapanthus produced a couple of toffees. She gave one to Stella. 'Come on,' she said.

Stella unwrapped the silver paper and put the toffee in her mouth. She nodded.

They closed the door of the school silently behind them and crept out into the misty night.

Twelve

*T*heir footsteps echoed as they made their way along the street. A few lights gleamed in the windows of the tall houses. The shadows between the street lamps were very dark. A man came stumbling along the pavement towards them, muttering to himself. He saw them and broke into song. They scuttled across the road to avoid him. A dog barked from behind a high garden wall, making them jump. As they turned the corner into the High Street, a dark shadow dashed past, making Stella catch her breath. A cat, perhaps, or a fox.

She told Agapanthus what she had overheard in Miss Garnet's study. 'I was hiding,' she said. 'I heard Miss Garnet talking to her brother. She was trying to get him to do something for her, I think. I'm not sure.'

'What's her brother like?' asked Agapanthus. 'I can't imagine Miss Garnet having a brother.'

'He looked just like her,' said Stella. 'Except with a moustache.'

'How utterly revolting,' said Agapanthus.

The grand shops in the High Street were closing. They passed groups of tired-looking shop girls making their way home.

'What will we do if we find Ottilie?' asked Stella. 'If we go back to school, Miss Garnet will put us all into her album again.'

'I know,' said Agapanthus. 'But what else can we do? We can't run away. Where would we go? If we went to my home, my grandmother would just send us straight back to school. She would think that Miss Garnet's album was utterly marvellous. She always wants me to be quiet and obedient. She wants me to be more like my sisters.'

Stella nodded. 'That's exactly what my Aunts would think. That's why they sent me to school in the first place. They were in the album themselves.' She thought about that for a moment. 'That does explain quite a lot about them, actually. Aunt Deliverance had *Wilful Disobedience* written under her name. The same as me. And she ended up being the Head Girl and winning prizes.'

Agapanthus groaned. 'We don't want to turn out like that.'

Stella went on, 'And I discovered what my mother did too. I found her picture in the album. It said, *Wilful, Wanton, Wicked. Run Away with an Unacceptable Person. Expelled.*'

'An unacceptable person,' said Agapanthus. 'Who was that, do you think?'

'Well, I did think it might be my father,' said Stella. She frowned. 'Maybe my mother ran away from school with him.'

'Who was he?' asked Agapanthus. 'Why was he unacceptable?'

'I don't know anything about him at all. I don't even know his name. All I know is my Aunts disapproved of him. Of course, they disapprove of almost everything.'

'Do you think he helped her escape from school? I wonder how she met him,' said Agapanthus.

'I don't know,' said Stella. 'But if that's what happened, I can see why the Aunts are so disapproving. And why she was expelled.'

Agapanthus whistled between her teeth. 'My grandmother would utterly explode if I got expelled. Well, perhaps we'll think of something. But if we can't run away, at least at school Ottilie would be safe from those men.'

'If we find her,' said Stella.

'We'll just keep looking until we do,' said Agapanthus with determination. 'We know she's at the fairground somewhere.'

They reached the end of the High Street and crossed Museum Square. The Memorial Fountain was quiet. Water dripped from the basin into the pool. The museum was dark. They followed the street around behind it, past the row of tiny shops, and began to climb up the hill to the fairground.

Groups of young men and women were strolling down the hill from the fair, arm in arm. Families were coming home, the fathers carrying the littlest children in their arms, the older children stumbling along behind, half-asleep. Light spilled from the open door of a public house. Street stalls were selling hot chestnuts and coffee and pies.

As they got closer to the fairground, they could hear the engines thumping and the jangling music from the steam organs. Fireworks shot up into the sky, red and gold and green. There was a loud bang and then another.

They pushed their way in through the crowds. The swirling mist and coloured lights made everything look as if it were floating. The horses and griffons on the merry-go-round seemed to swoop through the darkness like creatures from another world. Young men plunged down the tall, curving slide of the Helter-Skelter, hooting with laughter as they hurtled around and around and slammed into the ground.

In an open space near the swing boats, two men were fighting, throwing wild, swinging punches. Men and boys shouted and cheered as they swigged from tin mugs, their faces lit up from the coloured flashes of fireworks overhead.

Stella gripped Agapanthus's hand tightly as they made their way around the edge of the crowd.

People were coming out of the sideshow tents. The bearded lady poked her head out and looked up at the sky. She had a long, wispy beard and wore a midnight-blue turban decorated with peacock feathers. She saw Stella watching and gave her a wink before lacing up the tent flap and striding away.

'Look out!' Agapanthus whispered, and pulled Stella into the shadows around the side of the Hoop-La. One of the Gabbro brothers was shouldering his way through the crowd. He was carrying a large bundle wrapped in sacking over his shoulder and chewing a piece of cold sausage.

They watched him pass, then crept out of their hiding place and went on. They reached the edge of the fairground and made their way to the red-and-yellow wagon. The padlock was gone. Stella pulled the door open and looked inside. The wagon was empty. The walls were lined with wooden shelves. In a corner of the floor was a crumpled blanket and a tin plate and a mug.

'We're too late,' said Agapanthus with her hands on her hips. 'She's gone.'

Stella looked around. She tried to imagine Ottilie frightened, huddled in the blanket. She crouched down. Perhaps Ottilie had left a clue.

She spied something scratched into the wood, underneath the lowest shelf. It was too dark to see it clearly. She traced the scratches carefully with her finger. It was a drawing of a small garden slug.

'Look at this. It's her walrus.'

Agapanthus knelt beside her and peered underneath the shelf. She ran her finger along the scratched lines of the tiny drawing. 'You're right. That is her walrus, isn't it? But why didn't she write something?'

'Perhaps she was too frightened. She hid it under here, where they wouldn't see it.' Stella felt along the underside of the shelf. 'There's something else too. What's this supposed to be, do you think?'

Agapanthus felt it and frowned. 'It might be anything,' she said. 'Ottilie's utterly dreadful at drawing, isn't she? I wish we had a candle.' She ran her fingers over the scratches again. 'Well, it feels like a snake climbing up a tree. That makes no sense.'

Stella traced the shape with her finger. 'It's a tower, I think,' she said. 'Or a lighthouse. And this snake bit goes around — Oh! It's the Helter-Skelter, isn't it?'

'Well, it might be,' admitted Agapanthus.

'I think it's a message. A clue,' said Stella. She felt along the shelf for more scratches, but there was nothing. She stood up. 'Come on.'

They looked warily out of the wagon, climbed down and made their way back past the sideshows towards the Helter-Skelter. The fairground was beginning to close. The engines were slowing, banging and clanking and hissing steam. A man blew out the coloured glass lanterns around the entrance of a sideshow tent. At the Hoop-La, a girl was flinging the little toy camels and elephants and horses into a cardboard box.

'Git movin'.' One of the Gabbro brothers was hurrying people along. He was sucking on a marrowbone as he walked. 'Fair's closin'. Go on. Git on home.'

Stella pulled Agapanthus away from him, around behind the merry-go-round. They ducked down, watching him through the legs of the horses.

'We should hide until everyone's gone,' whispered Stella.

They found a dark corner beside a gingerbread stall and crouched behind a pile of empty crates, waiting as the fairground became quieter, the steam engines stopped and the lights went out. They could see the top of the Helter-Skelter. A row of red and blue lanterns flickered there in the breeze. The slide curved around, gleaming in the darkness. As they watched, a figure appeared at the top of the tower and blew out the lanterns, one by one.

A man walked past, whistling and carrying a tool bag, and then a group of young men, laughing. Three girls came by, wearing shabby coats over their spangled costumes.

At last, everything was quiet.

'Let's go,' said Agapanthus.

Stella gripped her arm. 'Wait!'

One of the Gabbro brothers strode past. They crept out of their hiding place and followed him cautiously, keeping to the shadows. He ran up the stairs of the Helter-Skelter and went inside.

Stella and Agapanthus ducked into the dark shadow behind the ticket booth.

After several moments, all three Gabbro brothers came out of the tower together. One of them closed the door and locked it with a padlock.

'That's done,' he said, looking around. 'So, boys. We go and tell him we got her hidden away somewhere secret, right and tight, and if he wants her, he'll be payin' us a bit more. A guinea apiece, this time.'

The other two laughed. One of them rubbed his hands together. 'It'll be oyster pies for us.'

'Pig's knuckles, all swimming in gravy,' said the third brother, smacking his lips.

They hurried away together, towards the entrance to the fairground.

Stella and Agapanthus waited until the brothers were out of sight.

Stella breathed, 'Let's go.'

They climbed the steps to the door of the Helter-Skelter. Agapanthus rattled the padlock. Stella whispered, 'Ottilie! Ottilie! Are you in there?'

There was no answer.

Agapanthus called, a bit louder, 'Ottilie! It's us! Are you there?'

A faint sound came from somewhere above their heads.

'Did you hear that?' whispered Stella.

'No.'

'I'm sure I heard something. Is there another way in?'

They climbed down the stairs and looked up at the tower.

'Do you think we could get up the slide?' whispered Agapanthus. She clambered up onto it, but only managed two steps before she came slithering back down, hitting the ground with a thump. 'No,' she said, frowning and rubbing her behind. 'Perhaps not.'

They walked around the back of the tower.

Agapanthus poked at the boards with the toe of her boot. 'It's rotten,' she said. She grabbed the lowest board, braced her feet and heaved. There was a crack and a tearing sound. The board broke. She managed to wrench part of it away. 'We could squeeze under there, don't you think?' she asked, panting.

Stella eyed the narrow gap doubtfully. She crouched down and peered underneath. The ground was soft and muddy. 'Maybe.' She lay down and squeezed her head and shoulders through. For a moment, she thought that she was stuck, but she wriggled with determination and managed to pull herself underneath the broken board, through the wet mud, tearing her stockings and scraping her leg.

'I'm in. Come on,' she whispered.

Agapanthus's head appeared. Stella grabbed her hands and helped pull her through.

'Ouch!' whispered Agapanthus.

They scrambled to their feet. It was very dark. Stella reached around and felt rough wooden scaffolding.

'Ottilie! Are you there?' she called.

Far above in the darkness they heard a squeak and desperate thumping sounds.

Thirteen

Stella and Agapanthus scrambled up the scaffolding to the entrance platform. Steep wooden stairs led up to the top of the tower. They began to climb, feeling their way in the darkness. The stairs creaked. Faint light filtered down from above.

'Ottilie!' called Stella. 'We're coming.'

There were more thumping sounds from overhead.

They found Ottilie lying on a landing, wrapped up like a giant cocoon. She had been shoved into a hessian sack and tied up with rope. They felt for the knots. Stella used her fingers and teeth and managed to loosen them. They unwound the rope and pulled the sack off Ottilie's head. She was making muffled squeaks. A handkerchief was over her mouth. Stella untied it.

Ottilie gasped for breath. 'Y-you came!' she said, and burst into tears.

'Of course we came,' said Agapanthus.

'Don't cry,' said Stella, patting her.

'I was so frightened. I didn't think anyone would find me,' said Ottilie. 'I thought that if I rolled over, I'd fall down the stairs. And also I think there are rats in here.'

Agapanthus said, 'Here, have a toffee.'

Ottilie unwrapped the silver paper. 'Thank you.' She sucked the toffee. 'W-we have to be quick,' she added, her voice shaking as she wriggled herself out of the hessian sack. 'They're coming back. They said they were going to get him, and then come straight back.'

'Get who?' asked Agapanthus, as they helped Ottilie to her feet. She was shivering. Stella put her arm around her.

'The gentleman, that's all they said.'

They started down the steep stairs.

'Who's the gentleman?' asked Stella.

'I d-don't know,' said Ottilie. 'It's been very strange. I don't remember what happened. I felt like I was asleep and just doing whatever they told me to. But then I woke up suddenly in that wagon. I tried to climb out the window and run away, but they caught me.'

'That was you, burning that page in the album,' said Agapanthus to Stella. 'That's why she woke up.'

Ottilie went on, 'They said you'd been poking around, looking for me, and they were going to lock me up here in the Helter-Skelter, and it wouldn't matter if I yelled, because n-nobody would hear me. So, I quickly scratched the pictures underneath the shelf in the wagon, just in case you came back. But it was dark, and I couldn't see what I was doing.' She sniffed and wiped her eyes. 'I didn't really think you'd find them.'

'It was a good clue. Very mysterious. Nobody else would have guessed that was a walrus,' said Agapanthus. 'Truly. Not ever.'

Ottilie and Stella giggled.

Suddenly, Agapanthus hissed, '*Shhh!* What's that?'

Footsteps were approaching. Keys rattled.

'They're coming back!' gasped Ottilie.

'Quick,' whispered Stella.

They turned around and clambered back up the stairs as fast as they could go.

Lantern light flickered. Huge shadows loomed on the walls of the tower.

They scrambled up and up, dragging Ottilie with them. She was shaking.

'Come on,' whispered Stella.

Heavy footsteps sounded on the stairs behind them.

They reached the ladder that led to the very top of the tower. Agapanthus went first, then Ottilie, then Stella. Agapanthus pulled Ottilie up the final few steps. An icy wind was blowing. The fairground stretched out below them, shadowy shapes and scattered, glimmering lights.

The ground seemed a long way down.

Agapanthus leaned out, looking at the top of the slide. It dropped away into darkness, impossibly steep.

Stella's insides gave a horrible, sickening lurch.

'We have to do it,' said Agapanthus. 'Don't think about it. Come on.' She snatched up a hessian sack from a pile nearby.

One of the Gabbro brothers appeared at the top of the ladder. He clambered up the last few rungs and lunged towards them.

Stella gasped.

Ottilie shrieked.

'Quick!' said Agapanthus, and she flung her arms around them, bundled them all together onto the sack, and leaped off the tower and into the night.

They hurtled down the slide. Stella heard a shriek, and she could not tell if it was herself, or Agapanthus, or Ottilie, or all three of them at the same time. Around and around they went, clinging together, plunging downwards. The wind whipped past, and the ground rushed up to meet them. They slammed into it with a thump that rattled their teeth. They tumbled over and over and staggered to their feet.

A man loomed out of the darkness and grabbed Stella's arm. She yelled and struggled. His grip tightened. Then a heavy body came hurtling off the slide and crashed into them, knocking them over. Stella rolled free. The men cursed.

'Come on,' gasped Agapanthus, pulling Stella up. They grabbed Ottilie's hands and fled, sprinting past the dangling flying boats and around the merry-go-round. At the entrance to the fairground, a large shape stepped out to block their way, arms outstretched, but they darted around its clutching hands and ran out into the street.

A coach was standing nearby. Stella had a glimpse of a dark figure inside it. Before she could think, they were bolting down the street. They passed the public house, diving between the people who were gathered outside, their feet skidding on the slippery cobblestones.

Behind, they heard shouts. The Gabbro brothers were coming after them.

Agapanthus looked back over her shoulder. 'This way!' She pulled them into a narrow alley between the houses. The ground was uneven, and they stumbled as they ran. They came out into a little court. A street lamp flickered overhead. Several alleys branched off in different directions. Agapanthus chose one that sloped steeply down the hill, and they continued running. On either side were tall warehouses. No lights showed anywhere. Something scuttled across the lane. A rat, perhaps. There was a smell of laundry and old cabbage leaves and something else, something nastier.

There were more shouts behind them.

Stella looked back. 'They're still coming!'

The girls ran on, stumbling down a flight of slippery steps and splashing through a drain. They hurried along a narrow, winding alley, gasping for breath, and came to another little court. On one side was a warehouse. On the other side was a high wall with broken bottles set along the top.

It was a dead end.

Footsteps were approaching. Lantern light flickered.

They looked around desperately for a way out. There was a small wooden door, but it was locked. Stella rattled the handle. Agapanthus banged her fist against the door, but there was no answer.

'Let me,' said Ottilie. She put her hand against the lock of the door and closed her eyes.

There was a little click, inside the lock. She pulled the door open, and they tumbled inside and slammed it behind them. Ottilie put her hand on the door, and they heard the lock click again.

They stood in the dark, trembling.

Something slammed against the door. They all jumped.

'Bleedin' lockwitch.'

'I flippin' told you.'

There were loud thumps on the locked door, and then grunts of disappointment, and cursing, and a few more thumps.

They waited. The men cursed some more. Then they muttered together for a bit. At last, their footsteps went away and there was silence.

'That was utterly astonishing,' whispered Agapanthus. 'How did you do that?'

Ottilie hesitated, and then whispered, 'If I touch a lock, I can open it. The locks want to open, really. They do. I can feel it. It's easy.'

'So you're fey,' whispered Stella, after a moment.

'S-some people say that.' Ottilie hesitated again, and then said, 'I'm a lockwitch. My mother too. All the girls in our family. My grandmother told me that her great-great-grandfather married a fairy lady. That's what she told me when I was little.'

Stella wondered if she should tell them that she was fey too. That she could turn invisible. Before she could decide, Agapanthus whispered, 'Well, I can see why they want you. If you can open doors as easily as that.'

'Those men came and took M-Mother away to do a job. They wanted her to open a lock. She was frightened — she didn't want to go. But she went, all the same. And she never came back. Something happened to her. That's why they want me now.'

'What do they want you to do?' asked Stella.

'I heard them talking. That gentleman wants me to open a lock. An underground door.' Ottilie's voice was shaking. It sounded as if she was crying again.

Stella patted her arm. 'We'll take you back to school. You'll be safe there.'

Agapanthus put her ear to the door. 'D'you think they've gone away?'

'I bet they're waiting for us,' said Stella. 'Perhaps we can find another way out.'

She reached about in the darkness and felt bundles and boxes. They were in a storeroom of some kind. Cautiously, they felt their way along, their outstretched fingers encountering feathers and fur, and rolls of fabric sewn with tiny beads. They passed shelves full of ribbons and jars of buttons and sewing thread, and emerged into a shop. Tall marble columns

were decorated with curly gilt patterns. A crystal
chandelier glinted in the shadows overhead. The long
counters were lined with plaster heads. All the heads
were wearing extraordinary hats. There were hats
with huge velvet bows, and dangling beaded grapes,
and exotic, spiky flowers. One hat was decorated with
a large pineapple surrounded by yellow roses, and
another had a whole stuffed bird perched on top of it,
the long green tail feathers trailing down behind.

They tiptoed across the gleaming marble floor to
the tall windows. Stella peered through a narrow gap
between the shutters. The street lamps flickered in the
mist.

'It's the High Street,' she whispered.

Outside, something moved. Stella clutched
Agapanthus by the arm. 'Look!' she gasped.

Something large and pale flapped past overhead
and disappeared into the darkness.

'What?' whispered Agapanthus. She put her eye to the gap.

'There.' Stella pointed.

'Where?' asked Agapanthus. 'I don't see anything.'

'There,' whispered Stella again.

'It's only mist.'

'I was sure I saw something,' said Stella. She watched the mist swirl, making uncanny shapes in the light of the street lamp.

'There's nothing —' Agapanthus stopped abruptly, and then gasped.

A stocky shape appeared on the pavement on the other side of the street. One of the Gabbro brothers.

'*Shhh*,' whispered Stella.

'He's looking for us,' whispered Agapanthus.

They watched him cross the street. They crouched underneath the window as he peered in between the shutters. Stella held her breath. She felt Ottilie trembling, and she reached for her hand and clasped it.

They heard him mutter something. He rattled the door handle. Then he walked away along the street.

They waited until everything was quiet.

'Come on,' whispered Agapanthus. The door was bolted and locked. They pulled back the bolts, and Ottilie put her hand on the lock and shut her eyes. There was a click, and the door opened. They edged out of the shop and closed the door. Ottilie locked it behind them.

Stella looked cautiously to the left and the right, her heart thumping. The light from the street lamps gleamed on the cobblestones. It was difficult to see in the darkness and the swirling mist, but the street seemed to be deserted. 'Let's go,' she whispered, and they tiptoed down the steps as silently as they could and made their way along the High Street, looking around all the time, keeping to the shadows.

They reached the end of the grand shops.

'Nearly there,' whispered Agapanthus.

'We can explain to Miss Mangan,' whispered Stella to Ottilie. 'We'll make her understand what happened.'

They turned the corner.

Something moved in the shadows beside a high garden wall.

Three hulking shapes stepped forward.

Stella gasped.

Agapanthus yelled.

Ottilie shrieked.

The Gabbro brothers laughed. One of them flung away a pig's trotter he had been chewing on and wiped his mouth with his sleeve.

'Grab 'em, boys,' he said.

Fourteen

'Run!' gasped Stella.

They spun around, but before they could escape, one of the Gabbro brothers snatched Agapanthus. The second brother grabbed Stella, yanking her arm viciously.

She struggled. 'Ottilie! Run!' she shouted.

Ottilie turned, but she was not quick enough. The third brother seized her and gave a sharp whistle.

A dark coach swept out of the mist. The coachman pulled the reins and the horses stopped, their breath

steaming in the cold air. Stella could see a dark figure in the coach. A gentleman. Ottilie wriggled and screamed as she was picked up and bundled inside.

Stella kicked and yelled for help. Her captor thumped the side of her head, making her ears ring. She struggled to free herself from his grip, but he wrenched her arm around behind her back. It hurt so much she thought she might faint.

Agapanthus thrashed and shrieked. The brother who was holding her slammed his hand over her mouth. She bit it, making him yell, and managed to wrench herself free from his grasp. She dashed to the coach and pulled open the door. The gentleman lunged towards her. They struggled in the doorway. The gentleman raised a walking stick, and Agapanthus snatched it away from him. He shoved her, and she fell backwards down the steps, into the gutter. She rolled over and lay still.

'Agapanthus!' Stella twisted and kicked, trying to escape.

Suddenly, there was a screeching yowl from overhead. It was the stripy cat. He dashed along the top of the high wall, fur bristling and green eyes gleaming. He leaped down, landed on the head of Stella's captor and clawed at his eyes. The man gave a howl of pain.

He let go of Stella and staggered backwards, thrashing his arms around. The cat yowled again, sprang away and disappeared into the darkness. Stella pulled Agapanthus to her feet. She was limping. She leaned on Stella's arm, gasping with pain.

The three brothers came towards them again.

With one arm around Agapanthus, Stella crouched and snatched up the fallen walking stick from the gutter. It was heavy, with a large silver knob on the end, decorated with curls and engraving. She grabbed the other end and swung the silver knob as hard as she could at one of the brothers. It struck his arm with a satisfying crunch. He yelped in pain and cursed.

'You've got to run,' Agapanthus whispered. 'As fast as you can. It's our only chance.'

'I'm not leaving you behind,' said Stella. Holding Agapanthus tightly, she backed away from the men, waving the stick at them in a threatening manner.

'You have to,' said Agapanthus. Her voice shook a bit. 'I can't run. When they grab me, you run as fast as you can.' She gripped Stella's hand and squeezed it tight.

'No —'

Suddenly, the three brothers swooped in. One of them snatched Agapanthus and wrenched her away.

'Run, Stella!' Agapanthus shouted, struggling as she was dragged towards the coach.

Stella swung the stick wildly. She banged one of the brothers on his jaw. He gave a yell and lurched backwards.

She swung the stick again. One of the brothers caught it, twisted it from her grasp and flung it away, over the garden wall.

'Haha,' he snarled.

Agapanthus was shoved into the coach. The door slammed.

'Go!' yelled one of the brothers to the driver.

The coachman cracked the whip, and the coach clattered away. As it passed, Stella could see the white faces of Ottilie and Agapanthus at the window. Sitting beside them was the dark shape of the gentleman. The coach swept away down the High Street, disappearing into the mist.

'We got the lockwitch,' said one of the brothers, panting. He rubbed his hands together, his knuckles cracking. 'Now let's finish this one off.'

They came towards Stella. One of them slapped his hands together with a sound like a gunshot.

Stella turned and fled. She sprinted back along the High Street as fast as she could go. She plunged down a dark side street and ran on, turned again and darted into a narrow alley behind the shops. She could hear the heavy footsteps following her. As she passed a flickering street lamp, she shot a glance behind and turned into another alley, ducking around piles of rubbish and empty boxes.

The alley came to an end. There was no way out.

Voices and footsteps approached. She backed around a pile of old crates.

'She's here somewhere,' growled a voice.

'Niggle her out.'

Stella crouched in the shadow behind the crates and tried to make herself disappear, but she was gasping for breath and her heart was pounding, and she could not concentrate. She felt her head swim.

Crash! A crate was pushed over. She jumped.

The men were close now. She could see their shadows, looming like giants, on the wall of the alley.

'Come on out, little girl, we won't hurt you,' said one of the brothers.

The other two laughed.

Stella took another breath and tried again to disappear, but before she could manage it, she heard a faint scraping sound. Not far from her feet, the iron cover of a drain lifted and slid aside. A round hole appeared. A pale face popped up out of the hole, and a voice whispered, 'Come on. This way.'

There was no time to think. Stella scrambled over and clambered down into the drain.

'Here,' whispered the voice, and she felt a hand guiding her feet onto the rungs of a rusty ladder. There was a scraping sound from above as the iron cover was pushed back in place. She climbed down. At the bottom of the ladder, her boots splashed into icy water. The air was damp, and there was a very unpleasant smell of drains and rotting things.

'This way,' whispered the voice. 'Watch your head.'

She crouched down and splashed through the water.

'Wait.'

She stopped, and there was a flare as a match was struck, and a small candle lantern was lit. In the glimmering light, she recognised Joe, the boy from the fairground. With him was a smaller boy. Both were barefoot, and they each had a hessian bag slung across a shoulder.

'We heard you,' Joe whispered, grinning. 'We keep an eye out for them Gabbro brothers. They're always up to no good. We heard 'em yelling, and so we come up to see. Then we seen 'em chasin' after you, so we come to the rescue.'

'Thank you,' whispered Stella. She took a breath

and looked around. The candlelight glistened on the wet bricks of a low, arched tunnel. They were standing in several inches of water. It flowed past silently, glinting in the candlelight.

'This is my little brother, Will,' Joe said.

Will grinned. He looked just like Joe, but smaller. He wore a patched coat, many sizes too large for him. It was belted around his waist with a piece of rope.

'I'm Stella,' said Stella.

'I know,' said Will. 'Joe told me about you. He gave me your wipe.' He waved his arm, and Stella saw her handkerchief had been tied around his hand. 'I got bit by a rat.'

'They get right big, down here,' said Joe. 'Big as bleedin' mawkins.'

Will grinned again.

'The Gabbro brothers took my friends,' said Stella. 'They were trying to catch me too.' She remembered Agapanthus's and Ottilie's white faces looking out of the window of the coach as it disappeared into the darkness. Where were they? How could she ever find them?

'Likely they won't follow us down here,' said Joe, 'but we need to keep movin'. Come on. Watch your head.' He led the way along the winding tunnel, ducking low, splashing through the water. They emerged into a wider tunnel, where they could stand more easily. There was a narrow brick walkway beside the water. 'Watch out, it ain't half-slippery, and you don't want to be fallin' in.'

'Where are we?' asked Stella.

'It's the sewer. We're scrappers, Will and me. We come down at night to look for —' He broke off and peered back behind them, holding up the lantern. In the darkness, something moved. They froze. Two green eyes gleamed.

'A rat,' whispered Joe. 'A flippin' big 'un too.' He dipped his hand into his pocket and brought out a pebble. 'I'll get him.' He flung the stone, and the eyes disappeared.

'You got to be right leery, down here,' said Joe, as they went on. 'You got to look out for rats, and for toshers too. That's why we come down at night, 'cos the toshers usually come in the day. And you got to watch the water, particular if it's been raining. Sometimes it comes belting down, right deep, and then you've got to run like the bleedin' clappers.' He laughed.

They crossed the stream on a slippery, wet plank.

'Careful.' Joe ducked under a pipe that trickled foul-smelling water.

At intervals along the walls of the sewer, words had been chalked onto the bricks. Will read them out in a whisper as they passed. '*Barrow Passage. Dog Leg Street. Salamanca Lane. Fiveways.*'

'Hear that?' whispered Joe over his shoulder to Stella. 'He's right clever, Will is. He goes to school. It's sixpence a week. He's learnin' all sorts. Readin', writin'. He's right quick at figurin' too. He ain't goin' to be a scrapper when he grows up — he's goin' to be a teacher.'

Will nodded. 'That's right.'

'He'll be a fine gentleman, sure as cheese, and he'll keep us all in fish suppers and oyster pies,' Joe said. 'And we'll be waltzin' all around the place in silk suits with pearl buttons.' He stopped walking and peered back into the dark tunnel behind them. 'What's that?' He held up the lantern. Their shadows made looming shapes on the curved walls. 'Somethin' is foll00win' us.'

Stella caught her breath. 'The Gabbro brothers?' she whispered.

Joe shook his head. 'I don't reckon. But it's somethin'.'

'Likely it's the fetch,' said Will. His voice shook a little bit.

'It ain't the fetch. Because why? Because there ain't no such thing,' said Joe. 'You're too old to be listening to them stories, you are. Likely, it's a rat. It's gone now, anyways. Come on. And keep quiet. We're right close to the Wake.'

They came to the end of the tunnel. Joe stopped and cautiously looked out into a dark, echoing space. Huge brick pillars supported arches overhead. A wide river emerged from a huge pipe and flowed past, rippling silently around the pillars, glinting in the lantern light, before disappearing into the mouth of another pipe. Mud banks stretched beside the water.

'This is the Wake,' whispered Joe. 'Come on. But keep dead quiet. And look out for trouble.'

They clambered down the wall, and Joe led the way across the mud to the edge of the water. 'It used to be a proper river, years ago,' he whispered. 'Fish and all. But now it goes in tunnels down here.'

There were pale lights moving in the darkness. Stella could see a dozen small, shadowy figures poking around on the mud banks. Each held a flickering candle.

'Do people live down here?' she asked.

'No, the air's bad,' whispered Joe. 'You can't stay down too long, you get sleepy, and you see things that ain't there. They're scrappers, like us.' He raised a hand to a small girl who was collecting sticks nearby, and the girl waved back. 'We just come down to find things.'

They reached the edge of the water, and Joe held up the lantern and looked around at the piles of rubbish

beside the river, tangles of sticks and rags and sodden paper. 'We're right underneath all them big shops in the High Street. We're looking for —' He stopped, crouched down and picked up something. 'Look.' He held out his hand. On his muddy palm were three tiny glass beads. 'Two blues and a red,' he whispered.

'Beads?' said Stella.

'They come from them fancy hat shops up above,' he said. 'They get washed down here when it rains. We pick 'em up, and our sister Liza makes them into flowers, and I hawk 'em in the street. Greens and blues and yellows, there's loads of them.' He dropped the beads into a little bag hanging around his neck. 'Reds too. The purples, you don't see them too much. Silver and gold, they're right rare, they are.' He grinned. 'Find one of them, and that's an oyster pie for supper.'

They went along the edge of the water, searching the mud. The tiny beads caught the light and glittered. Stella found a green bead and three yellow ones. She passed them to Joe, and he put them in the little bag. Joe and Will turned over the rubbish as they went, picking up sticks, pieces of wire and nails, bits of string, and the ends of cigars and stumps of candles, and putting them into the sacks they had slung over their shoulders.

Will found a small lump of coal and gave a whoop as he dropped it into his sack.

'*Shhh*,' whispered Joe. 'Stow that.'

The river lapped silently at the mud banks. Wisps of steam drifted from the oily surface of the dark water. Stella walked carefully, her boots squelching in the mud. She found a red bead and a blue one. She yawned and rubbed her eyes. Something glinted at the edge of the water. She lost sight of it as a shadow passed in front of the light, then she saw it again. It was tiny, gleaming like the inside of a seashell. She picked it up. 'What's this one?'

Joe inspected it in the light of the lantern and grinned. 'A pearl,' he whispered. 'A flippin' pearl. That's right lucky. That's a fish supper for all of us right there, that is.'

Will gave a hoot.

'Shut it,' whispered Joe, as he placed the pearl very carefully into the little bag and patted it. 'Keep lookin'. There might be more.'

Something moved in the shadows. Stella felt her heart lurch, remembering the creature from her dream. 'What is it?' she whispered, pointing.

'It's another bleedin' rat,' said Joe. He took a pebble from his pocket and bent his arm back to throw.

Two green eyes gleamed. The shape slinked closer. Stella recognised it and grabbed Joe's arm. 'It's not a rat!'

The pebble went wide, and the stripy cat emerged from the shadows and came towards them. He looked bedraggled and annoyed. He miaowed loudly.

'What's a flippin' cat doin' down here?' said Joe.

'He must have followed me.' The cat wound around Stella's ankles. She bent down and stroked his wet, shaggy fur.

'Is he yours?' asked Joe

'No,' said Stella. She picked up the cat. He bumped his head against her chin and bit her ear, quite hard. 'Ouch.' She rubbed her ear. 'Not really. He saved me from one of the Gabbro brothers. He leaped right on top of his head and scratched his eyes.'

'Did he just?' said Joe, grinning. He gave the cat a pat. 'You've got to keep him, then. What's his name?'

'I can't keep him. We're not allowed cats at school,' said Stella sadly. She remembered how she had found the cat on the roof, just after the clock had struck. 'Midnight,' she added. 'He's called Midnight.' The cat scrambled up onto her shoulder and arranged himself across the back of her neck like a heavy, and rather damp, fur collar. He dug in his claws and purred.

Joe patted him again and suddenly stiffened, listening. '*Shhh*,' he whispered, looking upstream, towards the mouth of the huge pipe.

A metallic, clinking sound echoed. Yellow lantern light flickered inside the pipe, glinting on the water. All along the mud banks, the little candles were extinguished and the scrappers faded silently into the darkness.

'Toshers, comin' down the Wake,' whispered Joe. He blew out the candle. 'Quick. We're goin'.' He and Will hurried along the mud bank, away from the water. Stella struggled after them, her boots sinking into the mud. She could barely make out their shapes in the darkness.

'What are toshers?' she whispered.

'They reckon all this, the Wake and all the sewers too, is theirs. Upstream, particular. They say if we go up there, they'll slit our throats and toss us in the water,' whispered Joe over his shoulder. 'And we don't want that.' He gave a short laugh. 'So we're leavin' now, quick. Come on.'

Stella glanced behind and saw several tall figures emerge from the pipe. They were wading through the water. They held lanterns and long sticks with wicked-looking metal hooks at the ends.

Midnight mewed loudly.

'*Shhh*,' said Stella.

Joe clambered up a crumbling wall, then reached

down and helped Will and Stella up into another narrow tunnel.

'Come on. Quick,' he whispered. They crouched down and made their way along, splashing through the shallow water. The tunnel sloped upwards. Water trickled down the brick walls. At intervals, dim light filtered from gratings overhead.

'*Sputters Lane*,' read Will in a whisper, peering at the chalk writing scribbled on the brick. '*Fishbone Yard. Lurking Cross. Rat Alley.*'

'Nearly home. Watch your head,' whispered Joe, as he ducked between the broken rails of an iron grating. They came to a rusty ladder. Joe and Will climbed up quickly. Stella followed them, clambering up awkwardly with Midnight clinging to her shoulder. She climbed out of the drain, took a breath of the icy night air and looked around as Joe and Will heaved the iron cover back in place.

They were in a narrow lane. A street lamp flickered. Dark buildings loomed up all around.

'This way,' said Joe, and he led them along the lane and turned into a court. They climbed down a flight of stairs and went along a winding alley. Stella stumbled along after Joe and Will as well as she could. They turned into a doorway and climbed a flight of stairs that wobbled and creaked. The air was close and smelled of sweat and dirt and boiled cabbage. A light gleamed under a door. They heard grumbling and a sudden angry shout from inside one of the rooms.

They went up another flight of stairs, along a passageway, then up another rickety, narrow staircase, almost as steep as a ladder.

At the top, Joe pushed opened a door. 'We're home,' he said. 'Come in.'

It was a tiny attic room. The ceiling sloped down to the floor in one corner. The gaps between the roof slates had been stuffed with rags. Pictures from the newspaper were pasted on the walls. In the middle of the room was a bed, and two little girls were asleep under a pile of blankets and rugs. An older girl was sitting at a small, crooked table beside the empty iron grate, making beaded flowers. A candle was alight, a pale, flickering flame. It was very cold.

'This is our sister Liza,' said Joe, pointing to the older girl. 'Lize, this is Stella. The Gabbro brothers were after her, so we brung her home with us.'

Liza smiled, but did not stop working. She had the same straw-coloured hair as Joe and Will. She wore an old felt hat, a patched, old-fashioned grey coat and a knitted scarf, and she had a piece of sacking wrapped around her shoulders. Beside her on the table was a row of broken saucers, each holding different-coloured beads, and a little pile of finished flowers. They glittered in the light of the candle.

Liza's face was scarred, and her eyes were milky blue. Stella realised that she was blind. Liza threaded several green beads onto a piece of wire and twisted them around deftly to make the leaf of a tiny daffodil.

'Stella's got a cat too,' said Joe. 'Midnight, he's called.' He said to Stella, 'Sit down here,' and pointed at a wooden crate beside the table.

Stella sat. She was sleepy and cold, and she ached all over. Midnight scrambled down from her neck and curled up on her lap, purring. She stroked his shaggy fur and thought about Agapanthus and Ottilie. They might be miles away by now. How could she ever find them?

'Any trouble, Joe?' asked Liza.

'No trouble,' said Joe. 'Toshers come, but they din't see us. But look what we found, Lize.' He carefully emptied the little bag of beads into a saucer, picked out the pearl and laid it in Liza's palm. 'Look at that.'

She rolled it between her fingers and tested it with her teeth. 'A pearl!' she said, smiling. 'That's a bit of luck, so it is.'

'Stella found it,' said Joe. 'She's right lucky.'

'Get your wet things off,' said Liza, 'and wrap yourself up, or you'll catch your death. Did you get something for the fire? There ain't no bread left. I gave it to the little 'uns, they were crying. But I saved a bit of soup for you. Put some water in — it'll go further.'

'We got some sticks, and Will found a huge great lump of coal,' Joe said. He and Will emptied their sacks onto the floor and sorted through the contents, pulling out a handful of sticks and the piece of coal. Joe laid them in the grate and lit the fire. The damp sticks hissed and steamed, then the flames flickered up. Joe poured water from a tin jug into a saucepan and put it on the fire.

They removed their wet coats and hung them up on a line that stretched across the room. Joe took a blanket from the bed and wrapped it around Will's shoulders.

'Take your boots off, Stella. We'll put them by the fire, and they'll dry a bit,' Joe said. He saw she was watching how Liza made the little flowers and explained, 'Lize was apprentice to a milliner, in the High Street. She was learning beadwork, she was right clever at it. But there was an accident, and she got burned and blinded, so now she makes flowers.'

'They're very pretty,' said Stella, as she unlaced her wet boots and pulled them off.

Liza smiled. She curled the leaves on the daffodil, laid it with the other flowers and picked up another piece of wire.

Joe poked the little fire and put Stella's boots beside it. He sat down next to Will and began sorting out the tiny beads they had found.

'So,' he said, spitting on a bead and rubbing it on a bit of rag. 'Why are them Gabbro brothers after you, anyways?'

'They took our friend away from school,' Stella said. 'We were trying to rescue her.'

'Asparagus? Your friend at the fair?'

'Agapanthus,' Stella said. 'No. Our other friend, Ottilie. The Gabbro brothers snatched her away.' She swallowed. 'We found her at the fairground, but they chased after us. We were nearly back at the school when they snatched her away again. And this time they took Agapanthus too. They pushed them into a coach. And the coach drove away with them.'

Stella felt tired and cold and very discouraged. She did not want to cry, but could not stop her voice from shaking. 'I don't know where they are. I don't know what to do.'

~ Sixteen ~

'Them Gabbro brothers are right bad,' Liza said. 'They were priggin' clouts and cacklers before they could walk, I reckon. Likely they've been hired to do someone's dirty work. What do they want with your friend?'

Stella hesitated. She was not sure if she should tell them how Ottilie could open locks so easily. It was a dangerous secret. 'Ottilie's mother was a locksmith,' she said. 'And a gentleman took her to open a special lock. An underground door. But something happened to her, and she never came back. And then the Gabbro brothers snatched Ottilie too.'

'Who's the gentleman?' asked Liza.

'I don't know who he is,' said Stella. 'And I didn't get a good look at him.'

'What was the coach like?' asked Joe. 'Was it from the fairground?'

'No, a gentleman's coach. It was black and shiny, with two horses.' Stella rubbed her eyes. 'It could have taken them anywhere. I don't know how to find them.'

'It's late. Have a bit of soup and get some sleep,' said Liza. 'And in the morning, we'll think what's best.'

Joe took the lid off the pot on the fire and looked inside. 'It's hot,' he said. He collected two tin mugs from the mantelpiece and carefully poured the soup into them. He gave one of the mugs to Stella. He swallowed a mouthful from the other, and then passed it to Will.

'Thank you.' Stella wrapped her cold fingers around the mug and took a sip. The soup was mainly water with little scraps of onion and potato floating in it. It was hot and comforting. She finished half and offered the rest to Midnight. He poked his head into the mug and lapped, purring.

Liza reached out and stroked his fur. 'He's a good size, ain't he?' she said. 'We could do with a cat. Mice, I don't mind so much, but big rats come up here sometimes, and I fret they'll nibble the little 'uns in their sleep. And black beetles too. I hear them scuttlin' about.'

'You could keep him, if you like,' said Stella. 'We're not allowed cats at school.'

Liza scratched Midnight between his ears. He rubbed his head against her hand. 'You stay at school, do you?'

'Yes. At Wakestone Hall.'

'That's right lucky,' said Liza wistfully. 'Learnin' all the time, and three meals every day.'

Stella sighed. She supposed that she was lucky to be at school. But she dreaded the punishments that would be waiting for her when she returned. She yawned and leaned her head against the wall. The little fire had almost died down, and the room was very cold. She shivered.

Joe stood up, took a rug and a blanket from the bed and said, 'Lize and the little 'uns sleep in the bed. Me and Will sleep here on the floor. You can share our rug, if you like.'

'Thank you,' said Stella.

Later, once Liza had blown out the candle, Stella lay awake in the dark and listened to the rain pattering on the roof. She rubbed her feet to warm them up a bit. Her toes felt like ice. Beside her, Will muttered something and turned over. One of the little girls cried out in her sleep. There were footsteps somewhere in the building. A door slammed. Outside in the street, someone shouted.

Stella thought about Agapanthus and Ottilie. Where were they? What was happening to them?

Midnight was curled up beside her, purring. She put her arms around him and buried her face in his shaggy fur. It was a long time before she fell asleep.

Stella dreamed again. She was very cold. She was singing. The notes swam through the misty darkness, like little silver fish. She was tired and very frightened, but she knew she must not stop singing, because if she did, something dreadful would happen. Beside her, a pale young man was playing a broken harp. The strings made hardly any sound, and his voice was no more than a whisper.

It was dark, but there was a glimmering, greenish light that seemed to shift and swirl. The air was as cold as ice and smelled of ancient things, long dead.

She sang on and on, and in the darkness around her, shadowy creatures flapped and slithered.

'Stella!' Someone was shaking her shoulder. She opened her eyes. It was daylight.

Joe grinned at her. 'Wake up, it's morning. You were singing in your sleep, so you were. You must've been dreaming.' He unwrapped a newspaper parcel.

'Buns,' he said, 'hot from the baker.' He passed them around.

Stella sat up. She was stiff and cold. The dream lingered in her mind. She could feel the creeping mist and almost hear the echo of distant music. She rubbed her eyes and blinked.

'This is Annie and Maisie,' Joe said, pointing. The two little girls were sitting side by side on the bed, wrapped in a blanket. They stared at Stella with serious expressions. They were thin and pale, with wispy, straw-coloured hair. Joe poured milk from a tin jug into a mug and handed it to them. With his mouth full, he said, 'I took the pearl down to Mrs Mackle at the shop on the corner, first thing, and she give me six bob for it. I told you we'd be rich.' He took a handful of little coins from his pocket and passed them to Liza. She counted them, feeling each coin carefully, and dropped them into a little bag she wore around her neck.

Joe said, 'So there's a dozen buns and a pint of milk, and I got a farthing sprat for your cat. And I got all our boots out of pawn, so I did. You can wear your boots to school today, Will, just like a gentleman.' He ruffled Will's hair, grinning. 'This clever lad is going to learn everythin' there is to know. And tonight we'll have a fish supper. We'll eat like lords and ladies, so we will.'

Stella was very hungry. The bun was delicious. It had a sugar glaze on top and was studded with fat currants.

Joe unwrapped a little fish from a piece of newspaper and gave it to Midnight, who wolfed it down in two bites, lapped up some milk from a saucer, and then washed his whiskers.

The little girls, Annie and Maisie, watched the cat with wide eyes as they ate their buns and shared the mug of milk between them. Annie put a timid finger out, touched his tail and smiled.

Stella remembered the musical box, and she took it from her pocket to show them. She wound it up and opened the lid, and the tinkling, melancholy tune filled the room. It sounded like raindrops falling on wet leaves. It reminded Stella of Luna singing. For a moment, she saw the darkness and the glimmering green light from her dream.

The little girls stopped eating and listened in enchanted silence with their mouths open.

When the music slowed down and stopped at last, Liza sighed and said, 'That was right pretty.'

Joe ran his finger over the smooth wood of the musical box, tracing the pattern of twining flowers. 'Who made it?' he asked.

'I don't know,' said Stella. 'It was my mother's.' She had never thought about it, but of course the box must have been made especially for her mother, because her name was part of the pattern, curving across the lid in silver letters. *Patience.* Someone must have made the shapes of the letters, and the leaves and flowers, and the tiny silver star and moon.

Liza sat up straight and said, 'Anyway, you'll be late for school, Will.' She passed him a bun wrapped in newspaper and a coin. 'Here's your dinner and a ha'penny for milk. Comb your hair and wash your face. With soap, mind.'

'Don't forget your boots,' said Joe.

Stella finished her bun. 'I was thinking about what to do.' She hesitated. 'Perhaps I should go and tell the police what happened, don't you think? They'll make me go back to school, which will be dreadful, but perhaps they can find Agapanthus and Ottilie.'

'We don't never talk to the flippin' peelers,' said

Joe. 'They'd clap us all in the workhouse, sure as cheese.'

Liza nodded. 'Likely they would. And Annie and Maisie wouldn't stand a chance. It's cruel in there for the little 'uns. We went in when our ma died, but as soon as I was workin', I got us all out again. The police would throw us back in, right quick. We don't tell the peelers nothin'. Not ever.'

Stella asked, 'What can I do, then?' She thought about the black coach driving away with her friends inside. Disappearing into the darkness. 'How can I find them?'

'I was thinkin' about it last night,' said Liza. She stroked Midnight. 'About that door underground and everythin'. It's right strange, ain't it? So, I reckon you should go and see Mr Cornelius. Tell him the story, and get him to tell your tea leaves. It's only a penny, and we can spare it.'

'That's an idea,' said Joe. To Stella, he said, 'Mr Cornelius knows everythin'. He lives in Coldwater Court, right over the way. He learned Will his letters and made us send him to school.'

Will was sitting on the floor, lacing up his boots. 'He gives me the frights,' he said.

'But he learned you all your letters, and he only charged a ha'penny a lesson,' said Liza. 'And when we din't have the ha'penny, he came and got you, and learned you anyway, din't he? And you learned them letters quick smart.'

Will pulled a face. 'They say he listens to what people are thinkin'.'

'You're too old to believe stories like that,' said Joe.

Liza said, 'He teaches piano and tells fortunes by looking at tea leaves. And he hears everything, all the talk about everyone. He don't miss nothin'. He's right clever. He knows about things. Everyone goes to him for advice.'

'It's true,' Joe said. 'He knows everythin'.'

Liza said, 'Go on, Joe, you take Stella up to see him. Here's a penny.' She passed Joe a coin. 'Wash your face. And comb your hair. You can leave your cat with me, Stella. You couldn't take him to see Mr Cornelius anyway, what with that bird of his. I'll look after him.' She stroked Midnight's shaggy fur, and he purred and bumped his head against her ear. 'We're gettin' along fine, we are. And mind your manners, Joe. Say good morning and thank you. You know what he's like.'

Joe nodded and stood up. 'I'll take you over, Stella. But I ain't staying. I'll wait outside. He's right scary, so he is.'

Stella swallowed nervously. Could Mr Cornelius be more frightening than Miss Garnet? Or the Gabbro brothers? It seemed unlikely. She took a breath and pushed the musical box back into the pocket of her dress. She pulled on her coat, shoved her feet into her damp boots and laced them up.

Seventeen

Joe took Stella down the stairs and out to a muddy yard, where there was a pump and a lavatory. They ducked under lines of washing. The lavatory was filthy. Stella used it as quickly as she could, holding her breath. Joe worked the pump handle for her to wash her hands and face with the piece of hard yellow soap, and then she did the same for him. Joe looked critically at Stella with his head on the side and made her wash her face again. 'He's right particular, Mr Cornelius,' he said. He took off his cap, pulled a broken comb from his pocket and ran it through his hair, patting it down into place.

'Come on, then,' he said, putting his cap back on. He led the way through a narrow passageway, under a crooked wooden staircase and into another court. All around, tall tenement buildings crowded together, leaning one against another. A drain trickled through the middle of the court. Hens pecked at the straggling weeds. Two women were pegging clothes on a line. A group of young girls was sitting on the steps, busy sorting tiny fish.

Joe said to Stella, 'Sprat sellers. They get 'em at the market, first thing, and hawk 'em in the street in the afternoon, at the back doors of the flash houses, for their tea. Oranges too, in season. Watercress. Walnuts. It's a good trade, but tough in the winter.'

They crossed a narrow street, where a pack of barefoot children were poking sticks into a grating. Joe waved at them, and the children waved back. He led Stella along a winding passageway and out into another crowded court. Several small boys and a dog were squabbling over a ball. Joe skirted around the game and pointed to the wall, where there was a neat, framed notice.

Alexander Cornelius

Pianoforte Instruction
Letters Written
Fortunes and Advice
4th Floor

'This way,' said Joe. They went into the building and climbed the dark, winding stairs, which smelled of damp and cabbage and washing. They passed a cluster of little girls sitting on a landing, tossing knucklebones. From somewhere above, Stella could hear a piano playing. They reached the fourth floor, and Joe hesitated for a moment, then took a breath and knocked on a door. The piano stopped.

'Come in,' said a voice.

Joe pushed the door open. 'Good mornin', Mr Cornelius,' he said, and pulled off his cap.

It was a tiny, spotless room, with windows on three sides, looking out at rooftops and chimneys and clouds. The shutters were open, and after the darkness of the stairs, the bright daylight made them blink. The floorboards had been scrubbed until they gleamed. There were birds everywhere. Sparrows were twittering and hopping along the mantelpiece. A blackbird was chirruping on the brass candlestick of the piano. A robin was perched on the little clock. As Joe and Stella edged inside the room, there was a whirr of wings, and all the little birds flew away out of the windows and were gone.

Mr Cornelius was sitting at the piano. He was thin

and elderly, and wore an old-fashioned dark suit, threadbare and neatly mended. On his head perched a jackdaw, a handsome bird with glossy black feathers and a sharp beak.

'Ah. Joseph. Good morning to you,' Mr Cornelius said. He stood up. The jackdaw flapped its wings to keep its balance on his head. 'Do come in.'

'Thank you.' Joe gave a little nod to the jackdaw. 'Good mornin', Nicholas.'

The jackdaw bobbed his head and cackled.

'I understand you had some luck in your endeavours last night,' said Mr Cornelius. 'How gratifying.'

Joe looked startled. He stammered, 'Y-yes, that's right, that is. Thank you. We found a little pearl. Stella found it. This is Stella.'

Mr Cornelius looked intently at Stella, his grey eyes alert. Something tugged at Stella's memory. Mr Cornelius looked familiar, but she was sure she had never seen him before. He reminded her of someone.

'How agreeable of you to pay me a visit,' said Mr Cornelius. 'Do sit down.' They sat at the little table. Mr Cornelius sat opposite them. He turned to Joe. 'How is Eliza, pray? And the little girls?'

'They're all prime,' said Joe. 'Thank you.'

'And how is William managing at school? I trust he is applying himself to his studies.'

'He is, that. He's reading, and learning all sorts.'
Joe hesitated nervously, and then added, 'Thank you.'

'That is most pleasing,' said Mr Cornelius. 'So, how may I help you this morning?'

Joe fumbled in his pocket and brought out the penny. He laid the coin carefully on the table. 'Stella wants advice, and her fortune told too.' He stood up quickly. 'I'll wait outside.' He bobbed his head to Mr Cornelius. 'Good mornin', and thank you.' He darted out, closing the door behind him.

Mr Cornelius smiled to himself and turned to Stella. There was something uncanny about his gaze. Stella could see why he made Joe nervous. 'Welcome, my dear,' he said. 'I will listen to your story, and I will tell your fortune. I will take the penny only when you believe you have received a penny's worth of advice. Those are my terms. Are we agreed?'

Stella nodded. 'Yes. Thank you.' She swallowed uncertainly. 'I hope you can help. I don't know what to do.'

'You will take tea.' It was not a question. Mr Cornelius stood up. His sudden movement made Nicholas cackle and flap his wings. He flew over to the mantelpiece and perched there. Mr Cornelius filled the kettle from a brass can and put it on the tiny fire that flickered in the

182

grate. He laid out two china cups and saucers, and spooned tea from a tin into a teapot that was decorated with a pattern of temples and gardens and little arched bridges. He crumbled a crust of bread and scattered the crumbs on the windowsill. Then he sat down again and said, 'Please, begin.'

Stella hesitated. 'It's a bit complicated.' She paused to think, putting the story in order in her head. She watched the sparrows flutter down to the windowsill and peck at the crumbs. She took a breath and began to tell Mr Cornelius everything that had happened since she had arrived at school. How Ottilie had been taken away. How they had found her note, and how she and Agapanthus had tried to rescue her, but had been trapped in Miss Garnet's album, and then Ottilie had been captured a second time and the Gabbro brothers had taken Agapanthus as well.

Mr Cornelius listened carefully without interrupting, his grey eyes never leaving her face.

Stella said, 'They were taken away in a black coach. A gentleman's coach. And I don't know where they are at all.'

'Good gracious. How very inconvenient for them,' said Mr Cornelius. 'And do you know what these men want with your friend?'

Stella hesitated again. Should she tell him Ottilie's secret? She met his steady gaze. She thought she could trust him. And she certainly needed his help. She took a breath and said in a low voice, 'She told us that she is a lockwitch. That's what she said. She can open locks just by touching them. And it's true. We saw it. She just put her hand on the lock and it opened.'

'A lockwitch,' Mr Cornelius repeated, unsurprised. 'That is a dangerous gift. Particularly prone to misuse. And her name? Ottilie —?'

'Ottilie Smith,' answered Stella. 'She said her mother had a locksmith shop, here in Wakestone. Her mother was a lockwitch too, and the men took her away, and she didn't come back. And then they came and snatched Ottilie.'

Mr Cornelius tapped the table with his finger. 'Smith. Of course. I recall the story. Perhaps a month ago, a little more. There was some talk at the time. She had the locksmith shop just by the market, not far from here. She went out, late one night, and she never returned. The police found no trace of her.'

'Ottilie was so sad. She was crying all the time at school.'

'No wonder. Poor child.'

'She said the gentleman wanted her to open an underground door,' said Stella.

'An underground door,' repeated Mr Cornelius. The kettle boiled, and he took it from the fire and filled the teapot. He seemed lost in thought, and he did not speak as he poured tea into the cups and passed one to Stella. The cups were made from china that was so thin it was almost transparent and were decorated with a pattern of ferns.

Stella picked up her cup and gingerly took a sip. The tea tasted of grass and dust. Mr Cornelius drank his tea slowly. Stella sat quietly and looked around the room. The sparrows chirped and fluttered on the windowsill. There were no pictures on the walls, but on the piano was a framed photograph of a young man. He was leaning against a plaster pillar. His expression was serious, but his mouth curved at the corners, as if he was trying not to laugh. Stella gazed at him. She had the same odd feeling as when she had first seen Mr Cornelius. The young man looked familiar. She felt that she had seen him somewhere before.

At last, Mr Cornelius spoke. 'Perhaps you know, many years ago, the river that flowed through Wakestone was covered over, and the grand shops and warehouses, the High Street and Museum Square, were built on top of it. The river still flows, but in tunnels underground.'

'I saw that,' said Stella. 'The Wake. Joe showed me.'

Mr Cornelius said, 'When I was a young boy, Wakestone was not much larger than a village and the Wake was still a living river. There were willow trees and rushes along the banks. I saw a kingfisher there once. Just a flash as it flew past. A brighter blue than the sky. I will never forget it.' He smiled. 'The village green was where Museum Square is now, just below the hill. At midsummer, the girls danced around a maypole on the green, beside the river.' He sipped his tea. 'It was a long time ago.'

Stella tried to imagine Mr Cornelius as a young boy. It was impossible.

'There were cottages around the green,' he went on. 'A forge and an inn. All gone now. Buried underground.'

'So, do you think that's where the underground door is?' asked Stella. 'Somewhere in the village that was buried?'

Mr Cornelius said, 'It is possible. I will look at your tea leaves. They will enlighten us, no doubt.'

Stella swallowed the last mouthful of tea, and Mr Cornelius took the cup, turned it around three times and placed it upside down on the saucer. He waited for the tea to drain away, and then looked inside the cup. His face became quite still. He seemed to be gazing at something far away, something Stella could not see.

'What is it?' asked Stella.

Mr Cornelius looked at her, and then back down at the cup. He turned the cup around.

'Please, Mr Cornelius. What is it?' repeated Stella nervously.

'Peril,' Mr Cornelius said. He nodded. 'I regret to say it is rather evident.'

He passed the cup to Stella, pointing to the bottom where the tea leaves clung together. Stella caught her breath. The tea leaves had formed into the shape of a monster. It had wings and long, spindly arms with thin fingers.

It was the frightening, clutching creature from her dreams.

Eighteen

Stella looked into the teacup at the shape of the monster. 'W-what is it?' she asked.

'It is the fetch,' said Mr Cornelius. 'There is no doubt. It is particularly clear.'

'What is the fetch?' asked Stella, frowning.

Mr Cornelius hesitated. Then he said, 'Have you seen it?'

Stella shook her head. 'No. Not really. In a dream, I think. What is it?'

'A creature from the old stories. People used to say the fetch came at night to snatch people and drag them down underground. When I was a child, my grandmother would warn me not to sing in the street after dark, because the fetch was attracted by the sound of voices. She told me stories of children who were shouting and laughing together at dusk, and suddenly they would look around and one of them was gone. And even now, whenever someone goes missing, people will say that the fetch has taken them. There have been a number of disappearances, just lately, and there has been some talk.'

Stella felt her heart beating in her throat. She thought about Luna. Had she been taken by the fetch? 'Is it real? Or is it just a story?'

Mr Cornelius said, 'There are those who still believe it.'

Stella asked, 'What does it mean, to be taken down underground? What is down there?'

'People used to believe that the fairies lived underground, inside hollow hills,' Mr Cornelius said. 'Perhaps it was true once. Fairies and dragons and sleeping armies. Here in Wakestone, there were stories about a giant's palace full of monsters and treasure, deep underground, below Wakestone Hill. The palace of the King of the Mountain.'

'A giant's palace? That's just a fairy story,' said Stella.

'As you say,' said Mr Cornelius. 'Stories such as these are still told to frighten children. If you are not home by nightfall, the fetch will snatch you and drag you down underground, and the King of the Mountain will eat you up.'

'It can't be true,' said Stella.

'Perhaps not,' agreed Mr Cornelius. After a moment, he said, 'In the old days, there was always much coming and going between humans and fairies. A baby was stolen and a fairy child left in its place. Children were enchanted and taken underground to work as servants, or fairy creatures came up to our world and fell in love. So now there are people who have a drop of fairy blood. A tiny bit of old magic. Fey, they are sometimes called, as I am sure you know.'

Stella nodded.

Mr Cornelius went on, 'I believe we understand one another. People dislike speaking of such things, and that is prudent, because there are dangers. People who are fey are often treated with suspicion and distrust. Some things are best kept secret. Your friend Ottilie has discovered this, of course.'

Stella nodded again. She knew that was true. She remembered Mrs Spindleweed saying fiercely, *Stay secret, stay safe.*

She thought about Ottilie, who could open locks because her grandmother's great-great-grandmother had been a fairy lady. And she remembered her friend Ben, from Withering-by-Sea, who could see visions in a pool of ink, because his grandmother had been part selkie. People with a drop of fairy blood. A tiny trickle of old magic.

Like herself. And her sister, Luna.

Stella wanted to ask Mr Cornelius if he was fey, but felt it would be impolite. Instead, she asked, 'What about —?' She hesitated. 'In my dream, I was underground, I think. It was dark, and there was a green light. And I was — I mean, there was music. Someone was singing.'

'Music? The fairies were always said to love music.' Mr Cornelius thought for a moment. 'My great-grandfather was a musician. He played the violin so beautifully that the fairies came for him, one night, when he was asleep. They took him deep into a wood and through a door that led underground, and they made him play all night as they danced. When morning came, he returned home. His family were overjoyed to see him. He had spent only one night with the fairies, but in our world, a whole year had passed. They had thought he was dead.' Mr Cornelius smiled. 'So the story went. And my grandmother used to say if you climbed up to the top of Wakestone Hill at midnight and lay on the grass with your ear to the ground, you would hear music playing, far below, in the King of the Mountain's palace.' He smiled again. 'I was never brave enough to attempt it.'

Stella did not know if she believed these stories or not. She looked at the creature at the bottom of her teacup. She shivered. 'Where are my friends, do you think? Are they underground? I think something dreadful might have happened to them.' She glanced out of the window, at the grey clouds and the roofs and chimneys of the town. 'They might be anywhere. I don't even know where to start looking.'

Mr Cornelius said, 'When I hear that someone wishes to use a lockwitch to open an underground door, and I see the fetch in the tea leaves, then this is where my thoughts go: it seems probable that someone is attempting to open a door that would be better left closed. And, if the fetch is indeed about, then I must suspect that door has already been opened.'

'But why?' asked Stella. 'Why would anyone want to do that?'

'Curiosity. Greed, perhaps. Where there are rumours of treasure, there are greedy men who wish to find it. As surely as night follows day.'

Stella thought for a moment, and then asked, 'If that's true, what do you think I should do?'

Mr Cornelius shook his head. 'I cannot tell you what to do. You must choose for yourself. There is peril, that is clear.' He hesitated, and then said, 'Sometimes the right path is also the most difficult one.'

Stella nodded.

'Let me see your hands.' Stella held out her hands, and Mr Cornelius took them in his own, studying her palms with attention. He looked at her fingers and the backs of her hands. 'There is strength here. And kindness. And courage.' He traced the lines on one of Stella's palms. 'I see twins. Does that have any particular significance for you?'

Stella nodded again, but did not say anything.

Mr Cornelius looked at her.

She swallowed. 'What should I do?' she asked again. 'How can I find my friends? I need to rescue them.'

Mr Cornelius smiled. 'Nobody can see the future. It is bound up with the choices we make. But if you are determined, then I can tell you that you held the clue here in your hand.' He laid a finger on Stella's palm.

'What do you mean —?' Stella stopped as she remembered the walking stick, with the heavy, engraved silver knob on the end. 'Oh. I hit one of the Gabbro brothers with the gentleman's walking stick. He took it, and then threw it over the garden wall.'

Mr Cornelius nodded. 'If you wish to find your friends, you must find that stick.'

'Yes, I see,' said Stella. 'Thank you.'

'Is there anything else you would like to ask?' said Mr Cornelius.

Stella shook her head. She knew what she needed to do.

'Do you believe you have received a penny's worth of advice?'

Stella nodded. 'Yes, I do. Thank you very much.'

Mr Cornelius started to say something, and then hesitated. After a moment, he said, 'Take great care, my dear.'

The jackdaw, Nicholas, had been dozing on the mantelpiece. Now he woke with a cackle and flew down onto the table. He picked up the penny, flapped back to the mantelpiece and dropped it with a clinking sound into a small box.

As Joe and Stella went down the stairs, they heard Mr Cornelius playing the piano again, the tinkling notes drifting down from above.

'I told you he was scary,' said Joe. He looked over his shoulder at Stella. 'Did he tell you anything?'

'Yes.' She explained about the walking stick. 'It belonged to the gentleman. The Gabbro brothers threw it over a garden wall. I need to go back and find it.'

'Easy as winking,' said Joe. 'I'll help you.'

'It was on the corner of the High Street, close to the school,' said Stella. 'It will be dreadful if someone sees me. Or if the Gabbro brothers come looking.'

'We'll turn you into a scrapper,' said Joe, grinning. 'They won't know you.'

Back up in the attic room, Stella told Liza what Mr Cornelius had advised her to do. Liza was busy making flowers and did not stop working, but she said, 'Take my coat, Stella. We'll mind your cat.' She nodded to the bed, where the two little girls were playing with Midnight. 'We're getting along fine. He's a good hunter, so he is. He already caught a mouse for his dinner and ate it right up.'

The little girls nodded solemnly.

Stella pulled off her own coat and put on Liza's. It was thin and patched and reached past her knees. 'Thank you,' she said, as she rolled up the sleeves. She hesitated, looking at the little girls, who were watching Midnight pounce on a piece of rolled-up newspaper. She lowered her voice to say, 'Mr Cornelius saw the fetch, in my tea leaves.'

'The fetch!' Liza gasped.

'There ain't no such thing,' said Joe.

'You don't know that, Joe,' said Liza. She added in a whisper, 'People say Mr Cornelius had a grandson what was taken by the fetch.'

'You shouldn't listen to stories like that, Lize,' said Joe. 'People go missing all the time. It don't mean the fetch took 'em. That girl from Crookback Court went missin' last week, selling onions at the market. Likely she just went off with someone. And a couple of scrappers went missin' a few weeks back. People say it was the fetch, but I reckon the toshers did for 'em.'

Liza shrugged and said, 'I heard that Mr Cornelius's grandson was a musician. He played the harp in the street, and at dances and that. And one day the fetch grabbed him and took him down underground. That's what people say. And that's why Mr Cornelius stays in that room there. He's waiting for his grandson to come back. Ten years he's been waiting, or more.'

Stella remembered the photograph of the handsome young man in Mr Cornelius's room. No wonder he was sad, if he had been waiting for so many years for a grandson who might never return.

Joe was bashing her hat out of shape. 'Maybe there were fairies and fetches, and who knows what else, back in the old days, but there ain't no such things any more.' He gave the hat a final thump and passed it to Stella. It was squashed and unrecognisable. She put it on her head.

'You look right different,' said Joe with a grin. 'Here.' He put his finger into the ashes of the fire and rubbed it against her cheeks. 'Now you look like a scrapper.'

'Good luck,' said Liza. She put out her hand and Stella grasped it.

'Thank you so much for all your help,' she said.

Liza held Stella's hand tightly for a moment. 'You be careful.'

Nineteen

Joe led Stella through a maze of narrow laneways and courts, past tenements and around the back of warehouses. They emerged on the busy High Street. It was misty and drizzling. Carts and coaches and omnibuses splashed through the puddles. They made their way along the street, in and out of the crowds, past the grand shops, and reached the corner where the men had captured Agapanthus and Ottilie.

'He threw the stick over here,' Stella said, pointing at the high garden wall.

'We can get over that, easy enough,' said Joe, eyeing the worn bricks. 'We'll go round the side so nobody sees us.' He led Stella around the corner, into a quieter street. He looked up and down. There was nobody in sight. 'Come on,' he said, and quickly clambered up the wall. He got his leg over the top, leaned down and held out his hand. Stella started to climb. It was not too difficult, although she was hampered a bit by Liza's long, flapping coat. She jammed her boots in between the bricks and gripped with her fingers. Joe grabbed her hand and hauled her up onto the top of the wall. From there, they could see a large house with shuttered windows. Just below them was a flowerbed full of straggling, wintry plants.

'Quick,' whispered Joe. They dropped down into the flowerbed. Joe peered out cautiously at the house. 'There ain't nobody home, I reckon.'

They made their way around the edge of the garden, keeping close to the wall, and came to an overgrown kitchen garden. There were rows of onions and Brussels sprouts, and cabbages gone to seed, and lots of tangled weeds.

'Where did they chuck it, do you reckon?' whispered Joe.

Stella looked up at the wall, trying to remember the night before. 'Over there, I think,' she said, pointing.

They began to search, pushing the weeds aside. Joe poked around in a big clump of leeks. Stella gingerly investigated a huge, dead artichoke plant with spiky leaves. There was no sign of the walking stick.

'It ain't here,' said Joe. 'I reckon somebody already found it.'

Stella looked up at the wall again. 'It might be over that way. Or maybe —' Then she saw it, above their heads, stuck in the branches of a tree. 'Look!' she said, pointing. 'There it is.'

'I'll get it down,' said Joe, and he picked up a stone and threw it hard. It hit the stick, which wobbled, but did not fall. The stone fell and smashed the glass of a cucumber frame. Inside the house, a dog started to bark.

'Oh no!' said Stella.

'Quick!' said Joe. He picked up another stone and flung it. The stick toppled out of the tree and landed amongst the cabbages. Stella darted over and snatched it up.

A tiny brown-and-white dog dashed from the side of the house, barking shrilly. It snapped at Joe. He scrambled up the wall. The dog turned and chased Stella. She ran around the cabbages and through the onion bed with the dog nipping at her heels. Panting, she reached the wall, passed the stick up to Joe and began to climb. The dog bit her ankle. She squeaked. The dog grabbed her coat and hung on. She fell off the wall, landing with a thump. The dog growled and seized one of her plaits.

'Stella!' gasped Joe, laughing. He reached down. 'Quick.'

Stella wriggled away from the dog, scrambled to her feet and clambered up the wall again. She grabbed Joe's hand, and he heaved her up on top.

The little dog jumped and barked.

A burly, elderly man came stomping around the corner of the house. He took the pipe from his mouth. 'What's all this, then?'

'Let's go,' said Joe. He looked down at the street and whispered, 'Flippin' heck.'

Just below them, two ladies with umbrellas had stopped on the pavement and were deep in conversation.

'Come on,' whispered Joe. 'Get ready to run.'

They dropped from the wall, startling the ladies. One of them gave a screech and tried to clout Joe with her umbrella.

'Quick,' he gasped. They dashed across the High Street, ducking between a carriage and a milk cart. The carriage horse whinnied and reared. There were shouts and the tinkling sound of broken milk bottles. Stella followed Joe as he sped into a laneway, skirted a cart that was unloading bolts of fabric and darted around a corner into an alley. He was gasping for breath and laughing. He looked around, and then leaned against the wall, clutching his middle.

'Oh,' he panted. 'I thought we were done for, so I did. Let's see what we got.'

They inspected the stick together. It was made of ebony, with silver bands, and a heavy silver knob on the end, decorated with scrolls and curlicues. There was writing engraved across the top of the knob. It was difficult to read because it was very fancy and curly, and the silver was worn and shiny with use. Stella followed it with her finger as she read it out to Joe.

Presented to
Thaddeus Garnet, Esq.
of Lantern Street, Wakestone
on the Occasion of
His Fortieth Year of Fellowship
of the Royal Guild of Artificers

'Thaddeus Garnet,' she gasped in surprise.

'Who is he? D'you know him?' asked Joe.

'Yes. Well, no. But I know who he is. I've seen him. He's Miss Garnet's brother. She's our Headmistress.'

'D'you reckon it's him what took your friends, then?'

'Maybe,' said Stella doubtfully. It seemed rather unlikely. 'Lantern Street. Do you know where that is?'

'It's the little street behind the museum,' said Joe. 'Bookshops and that.'

Stella remembered the street. She had noticed the bookshops the day before. 'Well, let's go and look.'

'Prime,' said Joe. 'Come on.'

Joe led the way through the winding back streets, swinging the walking stick as he went. They reached Museum Square and made their way past the fountain and around behind the museum.

Lantern Street was a narrow, cobbled laneway, overshadowed by the back of the museum on one side and the steep slope of Wakestone Hill on the other. They walked slowly along, looking carefully at the little shops. They passed two bookshops and a store that sold old coins. The next window had a crowded display of seashells, coral and fossils. They peered in, and then went on, past a shop that sold maps and prints, and another bookshop.

'Look.' Stella pointed at a hanging sign painted with fancy gold letters. She read it aloud to Joe.

Thaddeus Garnet, FRGA
Artificer
Scientific Instruments and
Mechanical Contrivances

In the window of the shop was a display of microscopes and telescopes and thermometers, and several other complicated devices that Stella did not recognise.

A little card was propped against a shelf: *Closed*. Stella tried the door. It was locked. She knocked, but there was no answer.

Joe peered in through the glass, cupping his hands around his face, then stood back and gazed at the upstairs windows. 'Let's try round the back,' he said.

A little further along the street, a narrow passageway led through to a lane at the rear of the shops. They walked along it, and Joe counted the doors. He stopped. 'This one.'

Cautiously, they opened the gate into a little yard with a copper boiler and a lavatory. They went along the brick path to the back door of the shop. Joe knocked, and then tried the handle. The door opened.

He whistled under his breath. 'Are we goin' in?'

Stella nodded nervously.

They crept inside, and Joe closed the door silently behind them. They stood and listened for a moment. They could hear a clock ticking and low voices upstairs.

Joe gripped the walking stick like a sword as they tiptoed along a narrow, tiled passageway. They passed a small kitchen and a flight of stairs and came to the shop. The walls were lined with shelves of scientific instruments. Behind the counter was a workbench. Tools were arranged in tidy rows. There were boxes and jars of screws and wheels and cogs. A microscope lay in pieces. A globe of the world was turning slowly, ticking and whirring, and a tiny moon the size of a marble circled around it. A cage of delicate, twisted wire held a little bird with real feathers and eyes made of black beads. A small mechanical crocodile, of brass and ivory, stood nearby. Joe touched it with his fingertip and jerked back in surprise when it lurched into motion, took two steps and opened its jaws.

A tinkling chime made them both jump. They spun around and saw a little door open up in the face of a clock. A mechanical spider scuttled out from the door, pounced on a tiny silver fly and disappeared again. The door snapped shut.

In a corner behind the counter was a desk piled with books and papers, several empty coffee cups and half-eaten meals. Stella tiptoed over to it and quickly leafed through the papers, hoping to find a clue as to where Agapanthus and Ottilie had been taken, but the scribbled figures and diagrams made no sense to her at all. She picked up an old leather-bound book: *Occult Subterraenia*. She turned the pages, but it was in a language she did not recognise. The tiny pictures were indistinct and unsettling. She closed the book with a shudder.

To one side of the desk was a large roll of paper. Stella glanced quickly over her shoulder at the doorway, then unrolled the paper and spread it out. After a moment, she whispered, 'Joe, look at this.'

Joe came over. He picked up a cheese sandwich from a plate and took a bite. 'It's a map,' he whispered with his mouth full.

'It's a plan of the town, like it's been cut through the middle, see?' whispered Stella. 'Here's us in Lantern Street, and here's the hill, where the fairground is, just behind. Here's the museum.' She pointed. 'Here's the main gallery. But look.' She frowned. 'There's a whole floor underneath. Storage, it says. And there's more down under that. Foundations. Look.' She pointed at a row of arched pillars, below the museum, sunk deep into the ground.

'What's this?' asked Joe. Rows of figures were scribbled in the margin of the map. Pencil lines had been ruled across, connecting the numbers.

Stella traced her finger along the lines. They came together below the lowest level of the museum,

underneath Museum Square. 'There must be something down there,' she whispered. 'We have to —'

'*Shhh*,' hissed Joe, clutching her arm.

A door rattled and opened on the floor above. Voices and footsteps were coming down the stairs.

There was no time to escape. Stella rolled up the map, and Joe shoved the sandwich into his pocket. They scrambled under the desk and crouched there, hardly daring to breathe.

Twenty

A man strode into the room. From their hiding place under the desk, Stella and Joe could see only his legs. He wore dark trousers and shiny black boots. He spoke, and Stella recognised the oily voice of Thaddeus Garnet. 'As I have told you several times already, Drusilla, I know nothing whatever about it.'

A woman followed him into the room. Her skirt swept to the ground. It was the Headmistress, Miss Garnet. 'I do not believe you,' she said. 'I could always tell when you were lying, Thaddeus, even as a child. I allowed you to take one of my girls, at some risk to my reputation. And now there are two other girls missing. What have you done with them?'

'As I said, I know nothing about it. And you assured me that the girl has no connections. So your precious reputation is in no danger.'

'That girl is an orphan and quite alone. Nobody will miss her. These other two are from good families. I was obliged to write to their relations.'

'Was that necessary? No doubt the brats have just wandered off. Consider this, Drusilla: their fees are paid, and you have two fewer mouths to feed. If they do not turn up, you can always say they died of a fever. Or tumbled down a drain. The world is a dangerous place.' He gave a short laugh. 'So extremely sad, you will say. Such a tragedy.'

'Don't be foolish, Thaddeus. The scandal would ruin my school.'

'That hardly matters,' he replied. 'In a few days, we will both be richer than you can imagine, and far beyond the reach of these petty concerns. Let me tell you, Drusilla, I do not intend to waste my remaining years here in this insignificant town, mending microscopes. I have larger ambitions.'

Miss Garnet sniffed. 'So you always say. Well, if, indeed, you know nothing about these two missing girls, I must go to the police.'

His voice was suddenly as cold as ice. 'That would be a mistake.' He stepped closer to her and did something that Stella could not see. It made Miss Garnet gasp in pain. 'No,' he said. 'I cannot have the police sniffing around. It has taken me years of work to get to this point. Believe me, I will make our fortune. But I cannot allow you to get in my way.'

'You do not frighten me, little brother,' said Miss Garnet, backing away from him. 'As a child, you were always devious and untrustworthy. You have not changed. If you do not have better news for me by tonight, I will go to the police, whatever the consequences. Make no doubt about that.'

She turned and stalked from the room. After a moment, the back door slammed.

Stella felt cold inside. She could hardly believe that Miss Garnet had allowed her horrible brother to kidnap Ottilie from school like that. *Nobody will miss her,* she had said. Poor Ottilie. Where was she? And where was Agapanthus? What had Mr Garnet done with them?

They listened as Mr Garnet paced around the room for a bit, muttering to himself, picking things up and putting them down again. He went out, and they heard his footsteps along the passageway. A key turned in a lock. Something clinked. Hinges creaked. They heard more footsteps, going downstairs. Then there was silence.

After a minute, Joe crept out from under the desk. He peered around the counter, clutching the walking stick, ready to run. Then he beckoned to Stella and whispered, 'He's gone.'

The passageway was empty. They tiptoed to the back door and Joe tried the handle. 'Locked,' he said.

'Look.' Stella pointed.

Underneath the staircase was a door, slightly ajar. If it had been closed, it would have been quite hidden in the panelling; they would never have noticed it. Cautiously, Stella pulled it open. A flight of wooden stairs led down to a cellar.

She swallowed and whispered, 'You don't have to come with me. If you don't want to.'

'I'm comin',' said Joe. He gripped the walking stick with determination.

They tiptoed down the stairs.

The cellar was dark and empty. Joe rummaged in his bag and pulled out the little candle lantern. He struck a match and lit it. In the glimmering light, they saw a low, arched opening in the corner of the room. They ventured into it and made their way along a narrow tunnel. There was a rumbling sound overhead.

'I reckon we're under the road,' whispered Joe.

The tunnel sloped downwards for a short distance and ended at a brick wall. Some of the bricks had been removed, making a hole. They crouched down and scrambled through.

Joe held up the lantern. 'Flippin' heck,' he gasped. Looming above them was a large stuffed elk and a huge stone statue with the body of a man and the head of an angry-looking bird. Crates and boxes and bundles were piled up in rows, stretching away in the darkness. There was no sign of Mr Garnet, or anyone else.

'I think we're in the museum,' whispered Stella. 'Underground. *Storage*, it said on the map. And there's another level under this one. I bet that's where he's gone. We need to find the way down.'

They tiptoed along, passing between huge crates packed with straw, and boxes tied with rope, and trunks pasted with labels in foreign writing. They ducked underneath the skeleton of an enormous lizard. 'Cop them teeth!' whispered Joe.

They went on. A large crate was leaking a greenish puddle onto the floor, and they skirted around it gingerly. They passed a marble statue of a naked gentleman holding the severed head of a giant. A bit further along, they came to a stuffed polar bear, a large bundle of spears and swords, and a pile of rusty helmets.

'Let's try this way,' whispered Stella.

They skirted around some suits of armour, turned a corner and went back in the direction they had come. Stella stopped and looked around.

'Are we lost?' asked Joe.

'No,' she said doubtfully.

They passed between rows of wooden crates and squeezed around the jawbone of an enormous fish.

On the floor, something glittered. Stella picked it up. It was a silver toffee wrapper. 'Agapanthus!' she whispered.

They went on and found another wrapper. They hurried along, scanning the floor. Joe spied another wrapper and then another one, gleaming in the shadows.

A little further along, Stella picked up another wrapper. She looked around in the gloom. 'Agapanthus!' she called. 'Are you down here?'

Somewhere nearby, they heard a thumping sound and a muffled squeak.

'Asparagus!' called Joe.

'Agapanthus!' called Stella.

They heard more thumping.

'Behind this crate,' said Joe.

He put down the lantern and the walking stick, and they pushed the crate as hard as they could.

It slid reluctantly across the floor with a loud scraping noise. Behind it was a wooden chest. It was locked. Joe looked around. Not far away was a pile of rusty weapons. He picked up a huge, curved sword and jammed the blade into the lid of the chest. He twisted the sword. The lock broke. They lifted the lid.

Agapanthus lay inside. She was curled up and had been gagged with a handkerchief. Her hands were tied behind her back. Stella undid the gag. Joe used the sword to cut the rope that tied her hands.

Agapanthus took a breath and sat up shakily. 'You found me!' she gasped. She clambered out of the trunk, grabbed Stella and hugged her hard. 'He said it didn't matter how loud I yelled because nobody would hear me. And, of course, I utterly yelled and yelled all the same, but I couldn't make any noise, because of the handkerchief, which tasted like old gravy, by the way, and nearly made me sick, and I absolutely kicked as hard as I could, but nobody came. It's been hours and hours.'

'We followed your trail of toffee wrappers,' said Stella. 'Me and Joe. Remember Joe? From the fairground.'

Agapanthus gave Joe a quick hug, and then she hugged Stella again. 'I dropped them, and I hoped someone would see them, but I didn't really think anyone would.' She wiped her eyes. 'It's been dreadful. I didn't think anyone would come. It was Miss Garnet's brother. Did you know?'

Stella and Joe nodded. Stella added, 'Miss Garnet let him take Ottilie. She said nobody would miss her.'

Agapanthus frowned. 'That's utterly dreadful. She's horrible. And he's horrible too. Like two revolting old toads. I'd like to shut them both in a chest. I'd fill it with spiders, though. Spiders and crabs. You don't have anything to eat, do you? I'm absolutely starving.'

Joe grinned. He took the remains of the sandwich from his pocket and gave it to her. 'It's cheese,' he said.

Agapanthus ate it in three hungry bites and said, 'Thank you,' with her mouth full.

'Where's Ottilie?' asked Stella.

'He took her down underground. He was taking me too, but I kicked them and tried to run away, so Mr Garnet told the Gabbro brothers to tie me up and leave me here, and nobody would even find my body. That's what he said. And then he laughed.' She shuddered. 'He just laughed.'

Stella patted her arm. 'We found you.'

Agapanthus nodded, took a breath and said, 'So now we have to find Ottilie.'

'Which way did they go?' asked Stella.

'This way,' said Agapanthus. She picked up the little lantern and led them between the crates, around several corners. She hesitated for a moment beside a huge, stuffed, hairy elephant with long, curved tusks, and then went on. 'Yes. Look.'

In a corner, behind a pile of wooden boxes, was a door. A sign read: *Do Not Enter.* The lock was broken, and the door was ajar. It had been propped open with the foot of a broken statue.

'He took Ottilie down here,' said Agapanthus, handing the lantern to Joe so she could pull the door wider. 'She didn't want to go. She was crying.'

Joe held up the little lantern. A rusty iron ladder led downwards into darkness. A cold breath of air came up from below.

'Do you know what's down there?' asked Stella.

Agapanthus shook her head.

Stella swallowed nervously. 'Well. Let's go and see,' she said, and scrambled onto the ladder and began to climb down.

ᴄᵉᵛ✧ Twenty-One ✧ᴄᵉᵛ

They climbed down and down, deep into the foundations of the museum. At the bottom of the ladder, Joe held up the lantern and they looked around. Enormous brick pillars reached up to the darkness overhead. They could hear trickling water and distant voices.

The ground was uneven and sloping. They made their way cautiously downhill.

'Look at that.' Joe stopped and pointed.

'What?' Agapanthus asked.

'Well, look. It's a street, ain't it?'

Stella realised what he meant. They were walking on cobblestones. A gutter ran down the middle of the street. They went on a little way, and Joe stopped again. 'That's a shop. And a tree. And that's an inn. Look.' He pointed to a row of crumbling buildings. The windows were dark and empty. Dangling chains held a rotten board that must have once been an inn sign. The pale, twisted roots of a fallen tree gleamed in the light of the lantern.

'The village that was buried,' whispered Stella.

'What's that?' asked Agapanthus.

Stella repeated the story Mr Cornelius had told her, as they went through the village, passing the forge and several ruined cottages. 'It was buried underground when they built Museum Square and the grand shops along the High Street. This must have been the village green, I think. And the river.'

They stopped on the bank and looked at the water. It flowed past silently, lapping around the remains of a ruined stone bridge, and then disappeared into the mouth of an enormous iron pipe.

'The Wake,' whispered Joe. 'I ain't never been this far upstream.'

'What —?'

'*Shhh*,' said Joe, cutting off Agapanthus. Voices were approaching. Yellow lantern light flickered. 'Toshers. Quick,' he whispered. He blew out the candle, and they scrambled down the muddy bank and crouched underneath the bridge.

Two men stopped and leaned on the parapet, looking down at the water. They held lanterns and long poles with sharp hooks on the ends.

'There ain't nothin' here,' said one of the men. 'I told you.'

'I heard somethin'. I heard flippin' voices, I did. And I seen a glim. Scrappers, I reckon.'

The first man laughed. 'Them scrappers ain't comin' down here. We knocked a couple of 'em on the head, and that put the frights on the rest of 'em, good and proper.'

The second man lowered his voice and jerked his thumb over his shoulder. 'What's he up to, anyway? All that burrowin'. It ain't natural. We ain't moles.' He looked behind and whispered, 'I reckon I heard somethin' singing. Deep down under. My nan used to tell me tales, when I were a nipper —'

The first man interrupted him with a crack of laughter. 'Singing? You're off with the fairies, you are. Talk sense. If a flash cove like that is payin' us to dig a dirty great hole into the hillside, then we dig the hole, and we get our chink.' He laughed again. 'We're done with digging now, anyway. We're to watch for anyone comin' up the Wake. And if they do, we'll slit their throats for 'em, nice and neat. Come on.'

The two men clambered down the bank and splashed into the river.

Stella, Joe and Agapanthus crouched, as still as stones, and watched the men wade through the water until they disappeared inside the pipe. Then they climbed silently back up the bank and made their way across the bridge.

On the other side of the river, the ground sloped upwards again. They crept between the brick pillars, keeping to the shadows. Ahead, they could see a faint glimmer of light. They tiptoed closer, as quietly as they could. They crouched behind a crumbling stone wall and peered out.

Just below their hiding place, the earth had been scooped out like an enormous bowl. Heaps of broken rocks and stones lay all around the excavation site. At the bottom of the pit was the dark mouth of a tunnel.

The three Gabbro brothers were sitting on stones, guarding the entrance of the tunnel. They were eating jellied eels from a newspaper parcel.

'Do you think Ottilie's in there?' whispered Agapanthus.

'I think so,' said Stella.

'We ain't gettin' past them,' whispered Joe.

'We could do a distraction,' whispered Agapanthus. 'And when they're chasing two of us, one of us could go in there and find her.'

Joe shrugged. 'Maybe,' he whispered. 'But I ain't likin' our chances, if they catch us.'

They watched the men for several minutes. The lantern light made their shadows loom and stretch into monstrous shapes. One of them picked something from between his teeth with a fingernail and flicked it away.

Stella took a breath. 'It has to be me,' she said nervously. She could feel her heart beating. 'I'm the only one who can get past them.'

'How?' asked Agapanthus.

'Like this,' said Stella. And she took another breath and made herself fade. She felt the familiar horrible, dizzy feeling as she disappeared, and she saw their mouths fall open in surprise. She let herself appear again. She was shaking. 'So, it has to be me. I can go invisible and get past them.'

Agapanthus and Joe looked astonished.

'That's utterly extraordinary,' whispered Agapanthus, after a moment.

'How d'you do it?' asked Joe.

'It's because ...' Stella felt awkward. 'It's because I'm fey.' It was very strange to say it aloud. She avoided their eyes. 'So, I'll go in there and see if I can find Ottilie.'

'Are you sure?' asked Agapanthus.

Stella nodded. 'And if I don't come out again —'

Agapanthus grabbed Stella's hand and squeezed it. 'If you don't come out, we'll come in and save you.'

'Sure as cheese,' said Joe, nodding.

Stella hugged them both. Then, before she could change her mind, she took a breath and made herself invisible again. Her head swam as she disappeared.

She stood up, climbed over the wall and began to make her way down the slope, towards the Gabbro brothers and the entrance to the tunnel. She edged down as cautiously as she could, one step at a time. About halfway down, her foot slipped and dislodged several small pebbles.

Below, one of the Gabbro brothers got to his feet. 'What was that?' He grabbed a lantern and held it up, his sharp eyes scanning the slope.

Stella waited for a moment, and then went on even more carefully. She reached the bottom and tiptoed towards the brothers. She crept between them; they were close enough to touch. She could smell them: a mixture of old gravy, eels and sweat. She could hear them chewing. The one with the lantern moved suddenly and brushed against her.

'What was that?' he asked, spinning around, his eyes wide.

He was staring right at her. Stella could see the lantern light reflected in his eyes and the little bits of eel jelly caught in the stubble on his chin. Her heart was beating so loudly she was sure he would hear it.

'I don't see nothin'.'

'I bleedin' felt somethin'.' He pushed the piece of eel he was holding into his mouth and chomped it up as he reached out, his stubby fingers clutching at the air just above Stella's head. She ducked.

'You're seein' things, you are,' said one of the other brothers. 'Stay down here long enough, and you start seein' all sorts. You're givin' me the frights, jumpin' like a bleedin' coney.'

'You weren't here when that flippin' thing was howlin' like a banshee.' The first brother looked nervously over his shoulder at the mouth of the tunnel. 'Fair turned my gizzards, that did.'

'Sit down and eat your dinner.'

Stella tiptoed past them silently and made her way into the tunnel. It was narrow and very dark and sloped down steeply. She cautiously felt her way along, clambering over fallen rocks. After a short distance, the tunnel widened out. A lantern hung from a hook, and by the flickering light she saw two huge bronze doors. They were ancient, pitted with rust and ornamented with rows of studs, each the size of a man's fist. In between the studs were patterns of curling lines and strange, leering half-human faces. The doors were ajar, just wide enough for someone to slip through.

Stella hesitated on the threshold and looked in. The air was dead and cold and smelled of ancient things. A faint, greenish light flickered, swirling and shifting. It was the light she had seen in her dream. She half-imagined someone singing on the edge of hearing.

'Luna?' she whispered.

A muffled sound from close by made her jump. She spun around. A small figure was sitting curled up against the door. It was Ottilie. Her arms were wrapped tightly around her knees, and her head was down.

Stella made herself become visible again and took a shaky breath. She knelt down. 'Ottilie!' she whispered.

Ottilie lifted her face. She was clutching the little toy rabbit that she had hidden under the floorboard at school. 'Stella!' she gasped. 'It's you.' She reached out and grasped Stella's hand. Her fingers were cold and trembling.

'Are you all right?' asked Stella.

'I've been so f-frightened.' Tears trickled down Ottilie's face. 'How did you find me?'

'We followed Mr Garnet. We found Agapanthus. She showed us the way down here.' Stella sat beside Ottilie and put her arm around her. 'What happened?'

'I didn't want to open it,' Ottilie whispered. 'I didn't. But he made me. It wants to stay locked. I can feel it.' She reached out a shaking hand and touched the door with her fingertips. 'It's very old. Mr Garnet made my m-mother open it. And he kept her here and made her open it whenever he wanted to go in. But then one time a m-monster came out, and it snatched her and dragged her in there, down underground.' She choked back a sob. 'That's what he told me.'

'The fetch,' said Stella. She patted Ottilie's shoulder.

'He said if I didn't do what he told me, he'd leave me here, and the monster would take me too. And he laughed.'

'What's he doing? Where is he now?'

'He's in there. He's finding treasure. That's what I think. He's got a heavy bag.'

'You've been very brave,' whispered Stella. 'And we've come to rescue you.' She hesitated. 'But I think I have to go in there too.'

Ottilie said, 'P-please don't go.'

'I have to,' said Stella. 'I had a dream about it.' She hesitated again. 'I think someone is in there. I need to find out. And rescue her, if I can.'

Ottilie whispered, almost too quietly to hear, 'But … Do you think there's a chance my m-mother is still —?'

'I'm so sorry. I don't know,' said Stella.

Ottilie bit her lip. 'I thought she was dead.' After a moment, she whispered, 'I'll come with you.'

'It will be very dangerous,' said Stella. 'Mr Garnet is down there. And the fetch too. And maybe the King of the Mountain, who might be a giant, I think. And I don't know what else.'

'Yes, I know. But maybe … And it's been s-so horrible, waiting here all by myself. I've been so frightened.'

'Are you sure?' Stella whispered.

Ottilie clambered to her feet. She wiped her face with her hands, took a shuddering breath and nodded. She pushed the toy rabbit into her pocket. 'I'm sure.'

Stella stood up. She gripped Ottilie's hand and led the way through the huge doors and into the darkness.

Twenty-Two

Stella and Ottilie found themselves in a huge cavern. It was difficult to tell how large it was — the ceiling was high overhead, lost in the shadows. There were tiny glimmers of greenish light floating in the air, shifting and swirling like fireflies. Long-dead tree roots twisted between the crumbling stones. It was very cold.

Stella remembered what Mr Cornelius had said about the fetch — that it was attracted to voices. 'We have to be very quiet,' she whispered.

Ottilie nodded.

They tiptoed across the echoing space and came to the edge of an enormous hole. The ground dropped away. Stella looked down and felt her insides turn over. It was like looking into an abyss. A stone staircase spiralled around the edge, down and down, into the gloom.

Far below, things slithered and flapped in the darkness. A snickering howl echoed from deep underground.

Stella swallowed. 'You could still go back, if you want to,' she whispered. 'It would be much safer, I think.'

Ottilie's face was white, but she shook her head.

'Are you sure?' asked Stella.

Ottilie nodded.

Together, they began to climb down the stairs. They kept as close to the wall as they could. At every turn of the spiral, they passed columns and archways. In a dark opening, they heard a crunching, slobbering sound, as if something was being eaten. Ottilie gave a muffled squeak as they tiptoed quickly past.

The walls were stone. In places, there were carvings of strange creatures. Some of the creatures' eyes were set with coloured jewels. Some had dark holes for eyes, where the jewels were gone.

Stella heard the singing voice again. She caught her breath. It echoed up from below. The notes seemed to swim up through the air, like tiny silver fish.

A shadow flitted past. They felt the flap of wings.

Lantern light gleamed. There was a faint clinking sound. They hesitated and went on more cautiously.

Mr Garnet was crouched on the stairs, chipping at

one of the stone carvings with a pair of pliers, gouging a jewel from the wall. He was wearing leather gloves and extraordinary brass goggles, with lenses of dark glass. He held up a sparkling red stone and inspected it in the light of his lantern, then dropped it into a bulging satchel.

Shadows seemed to flicker and cluster around him, as if attracted by the light. Something flew out of the darkness. Mr Garnet adjusted his goggles, turning a brass screw on the side, and watched as the huge shape flapped past.

Stella and Ottilie gasped and ducked.

Mr Garnet whirled around and saw them. 'What are you doing here?' He fiddled with his goggles. The lantern light glinted on the lenses, turning them into yellow circles. 'My own invention,' he said. 'They allow me to see things that would be invisible to others. Essential, down here.'

He lunged towards them.

Stella and Ottilie backed away, clambering up the stairs. Mr Garnet's hand shot out with unexpected speed and grasped Stella's arm. Brass claws emerged from his leather glove with a sharp click.

'Another invention,' said Mr Garnet.

Stella struggled, but could not pull herself free from his grip. The claws dug into her arm, making her cry out.

'Let her go,' said Ottilie, grabbing his arm. He shoved her away. She fell down, and he laughed. The sound echoed. In the darkness, something snickered. The shadowy shapes seemed to move closer, edging around behind him.

Mr Garnet gave Stella a vicious shake that made her teeth rattle and said, 'This is my discovery. I will be rich, and no little whining schoolgirls are going to prevent that. I need the lockwitch. For now. But I have no use for you. None at all.' He dragged her to the edge of the stairs. She struggled, twisting around, trying to pull herself free, but his grip was too strong. 'I don't know how you found your way down here. But you won't find your way back up again, believe me.'

He lifted her off her feet and flung her over the edge.

Stella screamed. As she fell, she managed to grab on to the crumbling stone at the edge of the stairs.

Her legs dangled into space. She clung on desperately and shrieked in fright.

Far below in the darkness, something howled.

Mr Garnet's strong brass claws began to prise Stella's grip away, one finger at a time. Her heart lurched in terror. She shrieked again.

A pale shape flew up from below. A hunched creature with long, thin arms and papery wings. It had tufts of wispy hair and no eyes. Its long fingers felt the air, clutching, snatching.

Mr Garnet stepped back with a curse. Stella clung on as the fetch circled, flapping overhead.

Suddenly, it swooped.

Mr Garnet screamed. The fetch grabbed him around the neck and lifted him off the ground. He screamed again, struggling. The fetch gripped him tightly and howled. Then it plunged down into the darkness and was gone. A bubbling screech echoed up from below.

Ottilie scuttled forward, grasped Stella's arms and dragged her to safety. They stumbled away from the edge and crouched against the wall.

Stella was shaking.

'Are you all right?' whispered Ottilie.

'Yes.' She felt as if she might faint. 'Maybe.' Her fingers were cut and bruised. Mr Garnet's brass claws had torn her coat sleeve, and her arm was bleeding.

Ottilie's face was pale, her eyes wide. 'That was horrible,' she whispered.

'Yes.' Stella swallowed. 'Yes, it was.' After a moment, she asked, 'Are you sure you want to go on?'

Ottilie hesitated, and then nodded. 'Are you?'

Stella took a shuddering breath. 'Yes.'

They stood up. Stella remembered Joe collecting stones to throw at the rats in the sewer. She picked up a handful of pebbles that lay on the floor and put them in her pocket. Then she clasped Ottilie's hand, and they continued down the stairs.

Tendrils of mist drifted and curled through the air, making it difficult to see. They passed clusters of pale toadstools glowing with a hazy, dim light. Stella felt her head swim. There was a horrible smell, of stagnant water and old, dead things. The air was as cold as ice.

At last, they reached the bottom of the stairs and found themselves in a large room. The walls were carved with intricate patterns and studded with glittering stones. Twisting columns reached up to the ceiling. Lights drifted through the air, casting a strange, eerie glow.

The singing was louder here. There were no words, just a high, whispery voice, beautiful and melancholy, like leaves drifting down from a tree. It swirled and echoed. It was difficult to tell from which direction it came.

A flock of tiny, fluttering things whirled overhead, hissing and chattering. Stella gasped, then dragged Ottilie through a doorway and around a corner. After a moment, they peered out. The creatures, whatever they were, had gone.

They went on, past dark doorways and stairs that wound further downwards, deeper into the ground. Something moved, and they ducked behind a pillar as a pale creature slithered past. It had a long, glistening body and too many legs. Its sightless head lurched from side to side. They waited until it was gone, and then tiptoed on, slipping through the shadows as silently as mice.

Suddenly, a deafening roar like a crack of thunder echoed along the passageway.

Stella gasped, and Ottilie gave a little shriek and clutched her arm. 'W-what was that?' she breathed.

'I don't know,' whispered Stella. She gripped Ottilie's hand tightly.

From somewhere ahead, they could hear faint sounds. Murmurs and low voices. They followed the sounds and came to a door locked with a heavy bronze padlock.

They peered in through the small, barred window and saw shapes in the darkness. Fingers clutched at the bars. A white face looked out at them.

Ottilie reached out and touched the padlock. Her hands were shaking. She closed her eyes. With a grinding creak, the lock opened. Together, they heaved open the heavy door. People stumbled out. They were pale and thin, and they looked dazed. An old man in a velvet coat, a young girl, three young men, a woman and a dozen more people. They stood and stared. Some of them sat down, bewildered.

Ottilie suddenly made a strangled, gasping sound. She stumbled towards one of the women. 'M-Mother,' she whispered, crying. 'Mother, I thought you were dead.'

The woman held Ottilie's face between her two hands and looked into her eyes. Then she pulled her close and hugged her tightly. 'My darling girl,' she whispered.

Stella peered into the cell. It was empty. She whispered to Ottilie, 'You need to get everyone out, back up the staircase. As quick as you can. You know the way. Will you be all right?'

'Of course,' whispered Ottilie. 'But aren't you coming too?'

'No, I have to go on. I have to find someone,' whispered Stella.

'I'll come with you ...'

'No, you need to save all these people.' She gave Ottilie a little push. 'You have to. You can do it. You're very brave.'

Ottilie hesitated for a moment, then wiped her eyes and nodded. She let go of her mother and gave Stella a hug. 'Good luck.' Then she took her mother's hand again and turned to the group. 'Come on,' she whispered to them. 'Follow me. W-we have to be quick. And as quiet as we can.'

Stella watched Ottilie lead the long line of people along the passageway, back towards the staircase. Then she turned and went the other way, in the direction from which the singing seemed to come.

She tried to make herself disappear, but nothing happened. She stopped walking, took a breath and tried again, but she could not do it. It felt as though the thick, stagnant air would not let her fade.

She hesitated nervously before going on, following the sound of the singing. She passed through an archway into a long room that was lined with glittering mirrors and crystals. The reflections made confusing patterns in the darkness. She tiptoed the length of the room and cautiously peered through a doorway.

It was the room from her dream. She caught her breath. A greenish light gleamed. Curls of mist drifted through the air. At the far end of the room was a looming shape, an enormous figure sitting on a throne. The creature was as tall as a house and looked as if it had been hewn from ancient boulders. On its head was a crown made of crystals and glinting shards of metal.

The King of the Mountain.

The mist swirled, and Stella saw a thin, young man. His skin was as white as paper. He was standing close beside the throne, and he was playing a little harp. The harp seemed to have only two remaining strings and made a faint twanging sound. The young man was opening his mouth, as if he was singing, but nothing came out. His eyes were closed. He looked pale and ill and desperately tired, but his fingers on the harp strings played on and on.

Beside him stood Luna.

Stella felt her heart beating. Luna was barefoot, and she wore a thin cotton dress. Her wispy hair hung loose around her shoulders. Her eyes were shut, and she was singing. Her voice was not loud, but it echoed around the dark space, filling the air.

As Stella watched from the doorway, the King of the Mountain pushed something into his gaping mouth and crunched it up. With one huge finger, he extracted a splinter from between his long, pointed teeth and flung it onto the floor. He took a swig from a bronze goblet. Then his head nodded, and his eyes closed.

Stella waited until she was sure he was asleep and crept into the room. Something cracked under her foot. She froze and looked down. The floor was scattered with bones. There were hundreds of them. Thousands. Some gleaming white, some greenish with mould. She gulped and carefully picked her way between them.

A bit further along, she stopped again. Her insides gave a horrible lurch. Lying amongst the bones were Mr Garnet's brass goggles and one of his leather gloves. She stared at them in horror. Then she took a breath and forced herself to go on. She tiptoed further into the room, keeping to the darkest shadows and as far as she could from the sleeping figure on the throne.

She reached her sister. 'Luna,' she breathed into her ear.

Luna did not stop singing. Stella reached out and grasped her hand. It was very cold. Luna gave a little gasp, stopped singing and opened her eyes.

'*Shhh*. It's me,' breathed Stella. 'I came to rescue you.'

'Stella.' Luna's fingers gripped tightly.

'Come on,' whispered Stella.

'I can't go,' whispered Luna. 'If I stop singing, he wakes up. And if he's hungry ...'

The King of the Mountain shifted and opened an eye. It was black and gleaming, like a stagnant pool.

Stella dropped to the floor and crouched in the shadows. She held her breath, her heart thumping in her ears, and watched as the giant's mouth opened, like a crack in a boulder. Pointed teeth glinted. He made a threatening, rumbling sound.

With a gasp, Luna started singing again. Stella waited. The giant's eye closed. After a moment, his head slumped forward. He began to snore.

How could they escape? They could not hope to run. The young man looked too pale and ill, and surely the giant would catch them easily in two strides.

The air was thick. The creeping mist curled through the darkness. Stella shook her head. Her thoughts seemed to be slower than usual. With a jerk, she forced her eyes open. She needed to stay awake and think clearly. What could she do?

As soon as Luna stopped singing, the King of the Mountain would wake up.

It was impossible.

Then Stella remembered the musical box.

She pulled it out, opened it and took out all the things — the little doll, the owl feather, the photograph of her family and the tiny strip of paper — and pushed them into her pocket. She fitted the key into the little hole and wound it round and round.

Luna was watching. She nodded.

Stella turned the key as far as it would go. She touched the silver letters of her mother's name, *Patience*, and the little silver moon and star. Then she looked at Luna and opened the musical box.

Tinkling notes poured out, echoing around the huge space, filling the air.

Luna stopped singing.

They watched the King of the Mountain. Stella held her breath. He did not move.

Luna gently took the harp from the harpist and laid it silently down. Stella put the open musical box on the floor beside it. They each took one of the harpist's hands.

'Come on,' breathed Stella.

Together, they crept from the room, picking their way carefully between the bones. The harpist stumbled along between them, his eyes closed. They tiptoed through the door and along the length of the crystal room, then through the passageways, towards the stairs.

Stella looked over her shoulder. Nothing followed them.

They reached the stairs.

Behind them, the musical box played on.

Stella and Luna began to climb, supporting the harpist between them. One step and then the next. Up and up.

Below, faintly, they could hear the musical box playing.

They climbed on, past archways and columns. Something flapped and snickered. Stella held her breath.

Far below, the musical box began to slow down.

They climbed as fast as they could, up and up.

The musical box slowed, and slowed some more.

They heard one tinkling note. Another note. Like two drops of water falling. And then there was silence.

Stella could hear their footsteps on the stairs.

And her own heart beating.

A long moment passed.

Then, far below, a roar rumbled like thunder.

Footsteps echoed, making the ground shake.

The King of the Mountain was awake.

Twenty-Three

Stella and Luna scrambled up the stairs as fast as they could, pulling the harpist along between them.

'Hurry!' gasped Stella. She put her arm around the thin, pale man. He leaned against her, his head lolling.

Heavy footsteps shook the ground. The King of the Mountain roared. It sounded like a train rushing into a tunnel.

They climbed up and up, gasping for breath. They staggered towards the final stairs. The huge doors were in sight. Lantern light gleamed.

Ottilie was standing in the open doorway. She beckoned. 'Quick!' she shouted.

Shadowy creatures leaped and flapped through the darkness, snickering and screeching.

The fetch swooped down with a howl. Long fingers clawed at Stella's hair, grasping her neck.

She shrieked and struggled free. She pushed Luna and the harpist towards the doors.

The King of the Mountain reached the top of the stairs. He towered above them, impossibly tall. He roared. His huge hand swept down and snatched Stella up into the air. His mouth opened. It was like a cave. Rows of pointed teeth glinted like shards of ice. His cold breath reeked of dead things. Stella screamed and struggled.

Suddenly, there was a bloodthirsty yell from below.

The giant lurched and dropped Stella. She fell to the ground.

A figure stood over her and waved two swords, one in each hand. 'Stella!' It was Agapanthus. She wore a large iron helmet with a red feather. The fetch dived, howling. Agapanthus slashed one of the swords at it, making it screech and dart away. She flung the other sword at the King of the Mountain, grabbed Stella's hand and pulled her to her feet.

'Quick!' shouted Joe. He also wore a helmet and wielded a huge axe with both hands. He lunged at the King of the Mountain's feet with a yell. The giant stamped and roared. Joe darted away, turned and swung the axe again.

All around, the shadowy creatures chittered and howled.

Agapanthus dragged Stella through the doors. Luna was there, holding on to the harpist. She gasped in relief and clutched Stella's arm.

Agapanthus screeched, 'Joe!' She waved her sword over her head. 'Quick!'

Joe threw the axe at the giant, then turned and sprinted to the doors. He flung himself through.

The pale people from underground were standing ready. They put their shoulders to the doors and heaved. The huge doors moved, creaking, and slammed shut with an echoing clang. Ottilie and her mother stepped forward, put their hands on the doors and closed their eyes. There was a deep thud as the ancient lock fell into place.

From the other side, something crashed against the doors, making them shake. There was a thunderous roar. Rocks began to fall.

'Run!' shrieked Agapanthus and Joe together. Everyone dashed along the tunnel through the falling rubble. Stella gasped for breath, jostled by the crowd, stumbling over fallen stones. They raced out of the tunnel. With a tremendous crash, it collapsed behind them.

The earth shuddered. Rocks rolled down the slopes of the excavation. One of the huge brick pillars shifted, toppled and collapsed. Great slabs of brickwork and rocks and dirt plummeted down. Stella and Luna scrambled over fallen debris, clambering upwards, dragging the harpist between them. They pulled themselves up and up, scraping their hands and their legs.

Dim light filtered down from overhead. The air was full of dust. They struggled on, climbing over the rubble. At last, Stella glimpsed the sky. She scrambled up into the cold air. She pulled Luna with her, and they hauled up the harpist together.

Stella took a breath, staggered a couple of steps, and then collapsed.

'Stella!'

She sneezed.

'Stella! Are you all right?' It was Joe's voice. Stella opened her eyes and looked up at the sky. The sun was setting, turning the clouds red and orange. She sat up and looked around.

She was in the middle of Museum Square. Beside her were Luna and the harpist. They looked dusty and bewildered. The pale people who had been underground were coughing and gasping and gazing up at the sky. Ottilie was standing nearby, smiling, with her arms wrapped tightly around her mother.

Agapanthus and Joe stood side by side, looking down at Stella and grinning. Joe pulled off his helmet and wiped the back of his hand across his forehead. 'That was somethin', weren't it?' he said. 'Asparagus and me came to save you.'

'We went up into the museum to get weapons,' said Agapanthus. 'Then we waited for ages for the Gabbro brothers to fall asleep. We were going to sneak up on them, bash them on the heads and tie them up. That was our plan. But then there was all this roaring and shouting coming from the tunnel, and the Gabbro brothers got scared, and they ran away. So we came in to rescue you.'

'You were just in time,' said Stella. 'Thank you.' She looked up at the sky. 'It's evening already.'

'You were down there for hours. Didn't you know?'

Stella shook her head in confusion.

'Time goes different down there,' whispered Luna.

'This is my sister, Luna,' said Stella. She reached out and took Luna's hand. Their fingers twined together. 'She was underground.'

Luna smiled shyly. She was shimmering a bit, half-invisible.

'She's exactly like you,' said Agapanthus, looking from one to the other.

'Except you can see right through her,' said Joe, grinning. 'That's somethin', that is.'

'It's utterly extraordinary,' said Agapanthus.

Luna appeared properly. 'I'm not used to bein' seen. But I can do it, easy enough,' she said.

'She was down there for ages, singing for the King of the Mountain,' explained Stella.

'I had to keep singing. When I stopped, he woke up, and if he was hungry, he ate someone,' said Luna. She shivered. 'The fetch brought them from the dungeon, or from outside, and he just swallowed them right down. It was awful.'

'He ate Mr Garnet, I think,' said Stella. 'I saw his goggles and his glove.'

Luna nodded.

'Serves him right,' said Agapanthus, frowning.

'Yes,' said Ottilie, sounding unexpectedly fierce. 'He really was horrible.'

Stella turned to the harpist. 'And this is —' She hesitated, the words catching in her throat. She was sure she knew him. She was sure she had seen him before.

'I reckon he's our father,' said Luna.

The harpist gave a weak, three-cornered smile. 'No. You're babies. Surely.' He reached out and took Stella's other hand. His fingers were thin and cold, but they gripped tightly, as if they would never let go. His voice was a whisper. 'I can see it. You look just like your mother. You both do.'

'I thought so,' said Luna. 'He's been playin' that harp down there, all this time. He's been playin' for ten years. He's been keepin' us safe.'

Twenty-Four

In the middle of Museum Square, where the Memorial Fountain had stood, was an enormous hole full of rubble. Water was seeping up from below, trickling across the cobblestones. Official-looking men in top hats, several policemen and a large number of curious onlookers arrived and stood around, talking and pointing and looking astonished.

The crowd grew. People stared at the thin, pale people who had come up from underground. An old woman suddenly gave a gasp, stumbled forward and embraced a young man. She held him close, crying. Another man knelt down and hugged a young girl. People were recognising their long-lost friends and family.

A large, smartly dressed gentleman in a silk top hat hurried through the crowd. He gave a loud laugh when he saw the old gentleman in the velvet coat, then burst into tears and pulled out a large handkerchief. He blew his nose with a sound like a trumpet.

An elderly man came briskly across the square. It was Mr Cornelius, with Nicholas the jackdaw perched on top of his hat. He stood and stared at the harpist for a moment. Then he said in a choking voice, 'Finn. My boy. At last.' The harpist stood up shakily, and Mr Cornelius stepped forward, put his arms around him and held him tight. 'I waited for you,' he said. He looked into his face and hugged him again.

The harpist said in a croaky whisper, 'Grandfather, these are my children.'

'Your children!' Mr Cornelius turned to Stella. 'When you came to see me, I felt … something, but I was not sure. I've been hoping for so long, you see. And you found him. Thank you.' He wiped a tear from his face and smiled. 'Goodness. This is not like me at all. Well, my dears, I'm your grandfather. Your great-grandfather, rather.' He reached out a hand each to Stella and Luna. On his hat, Nicholas flapped his wings and cackled.

The square was full of happy groups, and more people were hurrying in from the streets around to join them. The large gentleman was roaring with laughter. He gave a handful of coins to some boys, and they went scurrying away, coming back with bottles of lemonade and beer, and a fruit cake that was so large it took three of them to carry it.

Stella sat on the steps of the museum with Luna and Agapanthus and Joe, and her father and great-grandfather. Ottilie and her mother sat arm in arm, smiling.

Liza and Will arrived. Midnight the cat was riding on Liza's shoulders, and the two little girls trotted along behind her.

'Lize!' said Joe, standing up and taking her hand.

'Joe!' She hugged him. 'You're safe. I was that worried. You were gone for hours. I thought somethin' had happened to you.'

'I'm prime,' said Joe. 'We went down underground.' He guided Liza to the steps. 'Sit here, next to Stella.'

'Look at your cat,' Liza said to Stella, smiling and stroking Midnight's tail. 'He digs his claws in when I'm about to walk into something, and he hisses at people to make 'em get out of the way.'

'He's your cat now,' said Stella. 'He knows he is.'

'He fair bit a gentleman right on the nose, so he did, when he got too close,' said Will, grinning.

From Liza's shoulder, Midnight purred and eyed Nicholas in an interested manner.

Someone came past with a tray, handing out cake and bottles of lemonade.

Stella looked at the man she now knew was her father. He was sitting with his eyes closed and his pale face tilted towards the night sky. She studied the lines of his face. He looked thin and tired, but he was smiling.

Joe and Will went away and came back a bit later with an armful of blankets and a large newspaper parcel full of fried fish. They all ate the fish and watched the crowd growing. People were laughing and crying and talking. A hurdy-gurdy began to play, and little groups started to dance. Someone set off a firework, and it shot up into the sky with a bang and a whistle and a shower of coloured sparks. The crowd cheered.

Stella realised she was still wearing Liza's coat. She began to take it off, but then remembered all the things in the pockets. She took out the little photograph and the wooden doll, the owl feather and the tiny strip of paper.

'Look.' She passed the owl feather to Luna and the photograph to their father.

In the other pocket of the coat, she found the pebbles she had picked up underground. She was about to fling them away when she saw how they glittered in the evening light. Red and green, sparkling like coloured flames.

'Look at these!' she gasped.

'They're flippin' jewels!' said Joe. 'Rubies and emeralds.'

'The size of culver eggs,' said Luna.

There were eight of them. Stella turned them over and watched them sparkle.

'Cor,' said Will.

Stella smiled. She gave one of the jewels to Agapanthus and one to Ottilie. 'To remember us,' she said.

'Fat walruses forever,' said Agapanthus.

Ottilie laughed. 'Thank you.'

Stella gave one each to Joe and Liza. She gave one to Will, who grinned, and one each to the two little girls. They looked at her with wide eyes.

'Are you sure, Stella?' Joe asked.

She nodded. 'Of course.'

'We're rich. Look at this, Lize. We're flippin' rich, so we are. As rich as lords and ladies.'

There was one jewel left. 'We can share it,' Stella said to Luna.

Luna nodded. She was stroking the owl feather with her fingertip.

Stella sat back down beside her. 'What happened to Mrs Spindleweed?' she whispered.

'She died,' said Luna sadly. 'The fetch came for me, and she tried to stop it. She fought it. She tried to save me. She was very brave. But she died.'

'I'm so sorry.'

A tear trickled down Luna's face, and she wiped it away with a corner of the blanket. 'No crying, Tick. That's what she said to me at the end. No crying.'

'I saw it in my dream,' said Stella.

'I dreamed about you too.'

Stella took Luna's hand. Their fingers twined together.

Their father was gazing at the photograph of their mother and the two babies. 'This is how I remember her,' he whispered, almost to himself. 'I was playing the harp in the street, not far from here, and I saw her walk past with the other schoolgirls, and our eyes met. We fell in love. As easy as that.' He smiled. 'We were both eighteen. She was nearly finished with school. One night, she climbed out of the window, and we ran away together. We were so happy. We were going to see the world.' He touched her face in the photograph with his finger. 'But her family found us. Her sisters did not approve. And they took her away and hid her.'

Stella nodded. The Aunts would never have allowed their younger sister to run away with a street musician, however brave and good. They would have been horrified. Miss Garnet had written *Run away with an Unacceptable Person* under their mother's image in the album. No wonder she had been expelled.

Her father went on, in a whisper, 'I was desperate. I did not know where she was. I searched for months and months. And when I found her, I learned that she had two babies. Twins. Our children. I managed to send a message.'

'Midnight. Crossroads. I will wait,' said Stella. She unfolded the scrap of paper and showed him. 'Look.'

He took it from her. 'Yes,' he whispered. 'But the fetch was after me. And everything went wrong.' His voice was fading. He sighed and gazed at the photograph again.

After a moment, Mr Cornelius said, 'My grandmother used to say that generations ago, one of our ancestors was a sprite, and that's why music runs in our family. The creatures of the underworld crave music. They were always known to snatch musicians. That's always a particular danger for our family.

No singing in the street, especially after dark, she used to tell me.'

'What is a sprite?' asked Stella.

'They were the spirits of the air. Invisible creatures, with singing voices like silver bells, so beautiful that they could send people into an enchanted sleep.' He smiled. 'So the story goes.'

Stella and Luna exchanged a glance. 'We do that,' said Luna. 'Not so much the silver bells, I reckon. And I don't mind if I never sing again. But we go invisible. Me a lot, and Stella a bit.' She faded slightly, and then appeared again.

Mr Cornelius blinked with astonishment. He said, 'Well, that is quite remarkable. I never entirely believed the story. But it was true, after all. These things often come out with twins, I have heard.'

Their father took a breath and started to speak again. 'I knew the fetch was after me. I had tickets for a ship. We could escape her family, and the fetch too, and sail away. I sent her a message in the musical box, and I went to the crossroads in the wood every night, and I waited. I would have waited forever. But then the fetch came. I knew it would take the little children, if it could. So I led it away. It followed me, and it caught me, and it snatched me up and took me down underground to play for the King of the

Mountain. I played for as long as I could. I knew that as long as I played, my children would be safe.'

'She brought us to meet you,' said Stella softly. 'But there was a monster in the wood. It bit her, and it killed her. She was turned into stone.' She thought about the stone figure in the wood and the flowers that Luna had placed around her feet.

Their father gazed at them for a moment. He looked very sad. He whispered, 'And so I played and played. And slowly, I got weaker and weaker. Weeks went by. My harp was broken. And my voice was gone.'

'It weren't weeks. It was years,' said Luna. 'Ten years. Time goes different down there.'

He said, 'I did not know. I believed you were still babies. I believed I was keeping you safe. And then, when I could play no more, and the door was opened, the fetch went to find another musician to replace me, and they found you, Luna, and they brought you down to join me.'

'I was singing in the wood, when it came,' said Luna.

'Just where I had been.' He nodded. 'I am so sorry. I wanted so much to keep you safe.'

Luna patted his shoulder. 'We're safe now,' she said. 'We are, and you are too.' She looked at the hole where the fountain had been. Water had seeped up from below, forming a muddy lake. 'The door's locked tight and buried deep under all them rocks and water. The fetch ain't never comin' out again.'

Their father smiled and closed his eyes.

Twenty-Five

They all walked down the High Street through the town together. They stopped and said goodbye to Joe and his family, and a bit further along, they said goodbye to Ottilie and her mother. Then they turned the corner and walked along the street towards the school.

Agapanthus was frowning. 'I utterly refuse to go back in that horrible album.'

'It does sound rather iniquitous,' said Mr Cornelius. 'I will request a word with your Headmistress.'

When they reached the school, Stella and Agapanthus hesitated, but Mr Cornelius marched up the steps and rang the bell. After a few minutes, the door opened. The maid gave a little gasp of surprise.

'I wish to see the Headmistress, if you would be so kind,' said Mr Cornelius.

They were ushered into the entrance hall. Stella

and Agapanthus looked at each other nervously. Agapanthus pulled a face.

Miss Mangan came down the main staircase. 'Stella Montgomery,' she said. 'Agapanthus Ffaulkington-Ffitch. Where on earth have you been? Your behaviour has been absolutely disgraceful. Miss Garnet has written to your relations. What do you have to say for yourselves?'

Before Stella or Agapanthus could say anything, Mr Cornelius stepped forward. 'Good evening. I am Stella's great-grandfather. I wish to speak to Miss Garnet.' He tipped his hat. Nicholas flapped his wings and cackled.

Miss Mangan stepped back, looking startled. She hesitated, and then said, 'I will enquire.' She turned and made her way back up the stairs.

They waited. After a few minutes, Stella started to whisper something to Agapanthus, but she was gone. Stella turned around to Luna. 'Where is she?'

Luna shook her head. 'I don't know.'

Raised voices came from somewhere overhead. Someone squealed. There was a whoop of laughter and the sound of running feet.

Suddenly, Agapanthus came leaping down the main staircase, three steps at a time.

'What happened?' asked Stella. 'What did you do?'

Agapanthus grasped her hand. 'I nipped up the back stairs to Miss Garnet's parlour, and I snatched up that horrible album and threw it on the fire.'

Upstairs, the voices were getting louder. Someone yelled. There was a shriek and a tinkle of broken china.

They heard Miss Mangan call, 'Girls! Girls! Quiet there!'

A chorus of loud, giggling voices began to sing.

Wakestone Girls march on and on,
Doing just what must be done.
Never turn or flee in fright,
Always Righteous, Always Right.

The song ended with a squeal of laughter, and then dozens of copies of *The Young Ladies' Magazine and Moral Instructor* were flung over the bannisters into the entrance hall. They fluttered down like a flock of strange white birds.

Miss Mangan and Miss Feldspar were shouting. Miss McCragg was clumping and bellowing. And above the growing uproar came a high, shrieking wail from Miss Garnet.

Agapanthus gave a snort of laughter.

The doorbell rang, and a giggling maid appeared and opened the door. A large coach stood in the street outside. Its door opened, and Stella caught her breath. Aunt Condolence tottered out, followed by Aunt Temperance and Ada. The coachman unstrapped a Bath chair from the back of the coach. Ada helped Aunt Deliverance into it. She tucked the blankets around her.

Stella hesitated, and then went out onto the steps. Aunt Deliverance glared at her. She beckoned with an imperious finger. 'Come here at once!' her voice boomed. Her beady black eyes were like angry currants in a suet pudding. Stella felt the familiar sinking feeling.

'Stand up straight. Feet together. You look a complete disgrace. Have you lost all sense of propriety? Miss Garnet wrote to us. The mortification. We have come to collect you,' said Aunt Deliverance. 'Your behaviour has been completely unforgivable.'

'Inexcusable!' said Aunt Temperance.

'Deplorable!' said Aunt Condolence.

Stella looked at her angry Aunts. She supposed that it was probably too much to hope that Agapanthus burning Miss Garnet's album would make any difference to them. They had been dreadful for years and years — they were not going to change now. She said, 'Aunt Deliverance, please let me introduce you to my sister, Luna. And this is my father, Finn.

And this is my great-grandfather, Mr Cornelius.'
She beckoned them down the steps. Luna gave a little
bob. Their father bowed, and Mr Cornelius lifted his
hat. Nicholas flapped his wings.

'And that is Nicholas,' said Stella, pointing. 'He is
a jackdaw.'

Aunt Deliverance opened her mouth, and then shut
it. She opened it again, but only a faint wheezing sound
came out. Aunt Temperance's wandering eye circled
madly. She made a series of startled, squeaking sounds.
Aunt Condolence gasped for breath. She clutched at
her middle, and her Particular Patent Corset gave a
loud twang.

'Thank you for coming to get me,' went on
Stella. 'And for everything you have done for me.
I am sorry for all the trouble I have caused you.' She
looked at her father and said, 'But I will stay with my
father now.'

For a long moment, Aunt Deliverance just glared
and said nothing. Then she gave one quick nod.
'Well,' she said. Her mouth twitched. It was almost
a smile.

Stella blinked. Surely she had been mistaken. She
had never seen Aunt Deliverance smile. Not once.

Aunt Deliverance gestured to Ada to help her
back into the coach. Stella watched Aunt Condolence

and Aunt Temperance climb in after her. The coachman lifted the Bath chair up and strapped it into place.

Stella waved. Ada gave her a grim, approving nod. The Aunts frowned. The coachman flicked the reins, and the coach drove away.

Mr Cornelius arranged for Stella's trunk to be sent to his home. He tipped his hat to Miss Mangan, who was looking completely agitated and flustered by the sounds of commotion throughout the school. They said goodbye to Agapanthus, who was looking quite pleased with herself. As they left the school, a window was flung open on the third floor, and two girls poked out their heads. They were screeching with laughter and thumping each other with a pillow. The pillow split open, and the feathers burst out like a flurry of snowflakes.

Then they walked home together through the town. Stella and Luna held their father's hands.

'I hardly remember our mother at all,' said Stella quietly.

'I remember her singing,' said Luna. 'And I remember her crying. That's all.'

'She was very brave, and very kind, always,' said their father. 'And to me, she was beautiful.'

Stella sighed. 'It's sad we left her musical box underground. It was the only thing of hers that I ever had. It was lovely.'

Their father smiled. 'I made it for her,' he said, 'and it saved our lives. She would have been happy about that.'

'You made it!' said Stella.

'Of course. I made it for your mother, and for you as well. I put all your names on it.'

'It said *Patience* on it,' said Luna doubtfully.

'Yes. And there was a star and a moon. For Stella and Luna.' He stopped walking. 'When I heard two girls had been born, I knew what names she would have chosen for you. She named you after the night we ran away together. Stella for star, and Luna for moon. We talked about it that night.' He smiled again and looked up at the sky. 'See.'

The dark sky was cloudy, but high overhead were a thin crescent moon and a solitary, glimmering star.

Mr Cornelius made beds for them on the floor of his room with rugs and blankets. Stella was very tired, but could not sleep. It was warm under the blankets. She lay there, looking out of the windows at the night sky, and listened to her family sleeping.

She had so much to think about. So much had happened.

She dozed and woke again. Hours passed. At last, the sky outside lightened. She wrapped herself in a blanket and went to the window to watch the sun come up. Wakestone Hill was a looming dark shape. She thought about the King of the Mountain deep underground. She shivered and wrapped the blanket more tightly around her shoulders.

'It's beautiful, is it not?' said Mr Cornelius. He came to stand beside her.

Stella nodded. The sky gleamed like a candle flame. They watched the edges of the clouds turn yellow and orange.

'Have you thought at all about what you will do now?' he asked.

Stella felt in her pocket and found the ruby that she had picked up underground. 'Will this be enough for tickets on a ship? For all of us?'

'Certainly,' said Mr Cornelius. 'More than enough.' After a moment, he asked, 'Where will we go?'

Stella looked out at the distant hills beyond the town, hazy in the morning light. She remembered her beloved Atlas. When she had lived at Withering-by-Sea, she had spent hours and hours looking at the maps, and tracing her finger along roads and rivers and across oceans. There were so many places she would like to go. She wanted to see cities where people spoke in different languages. She wanted to see jungles full of tigers and elephants and parrots. Temples and towers and mountains and glaciers.

She wanted to see everything.

'Our cousins are in the Sargasso Sea, looking for seaweeds,' she said. 'Perhaps we could go there.' She held the ruby up to the sky. It sparkled in the light of the rising sun. 'To begin with, anyway.'

Three weeks later, it was raining when they reached the docks. They made their way through the busy crowd and climbed aboard the steamer. The porters carried their trunks aboard. The sailors cast off the ropes. People were calling out and waving goodbye. The river water swirled, grey and blue, glittering where a shaft of sunshine shone through a break in the clouds. Seagulls cried.

Stella leaned on the railing as the steamer moved out into the river. She stood and watched until all she could see of the land was a grey shape, far behind. At last, she turned away from the railing and walked across the deck to where her sister, her father and her great-grandfather stood. Nicholas was perched on Mr Cornelius's hat. He cackled and flapped his wings.

She joined her family and took hold of Luna's hand. Their fingers twined together, gripping tightly.

They stood side by side and looked ahead, towards the lighthouse that marked the line of breaking waves where the river met the sea, and to the wide ocean beyond, and they did not look back.

Acknowledgements

I'd like to thank my brother Steve for taking me to visit the beautiful Victorian pumping station at Crossness and for introducing me to the fat walrus. My sister, my neighbours and my friends for listening to all my writing problems — thank you for never telling me to shut up, or to give up. A big thank you to everyone who has worked on this book: Chris Kunz, Tegan Morrison and all the lovely people at ABC Books, especially Chren Byng, Kate Burnitt, Cristina Cappelluto, Hazel Lam and Kelli Lonergan, and to my agent Jill Corcoran. Thank you to Varuna the National Writers' House. And a big, extra-special thank you to all the readers who have followed Stella's adventures.

Judith Rossell is a writer and illustrator of children's books. When she is not working, she practises her dance steps, sharpens her collection of hat pins and stages *tableaux vivants* of famous sea battles in her fish pond. She lives in Melbourne, Australia.

www.judithrossell.com